From the Log of the Velsa

You are holding a reproduction of an original work that is in the public domain in the United States of America, and possibly other countries.You may freely copy and distribute this work as no entity (individual or corporate) has a copyright on the body of the work.This book may contain prior copyright references, and library stamps (as most of these works were scanned from library copies).These have been scanned and retained as part of the historical artifact.

This book may have occasional imperfections such as missing or blurred pages, poor pictures, errant marks, etc. that were either part of the original artifact, or were introduced by the scanning process. We believe this work is culturally important, and despite the imperfections, have elected to bring it back into print as part of our continuing commitment to the preservation of printed works worldwide. We appreciate your understanding of the imperfections in the preservation process, and hope you enjoy this valuable book.

US. FROM A PAINTING BY ARNOLD BENNETT

FROM THE LOG OF THE *VELSA*

BY
ARNOLD BENNETT

PICTURES BY
E. A. RICKARDS
AND A FRONTISPIECE BY
THE AUTHOR

NEW YORK
THE CENTURY CO.
1914

Copyright, 1914, by
The Century Co.

Published, October, 1914

CONTENTS

PART I—HOLLAND

CHAPTER		PAGE
I	VOYAGING ON THE CANALS	3
II	DUTCH LEISURE	24
III	DUTCH WORK	39
IV	THE ZUYDER ZEE	53
V	SOME TOWNS	70
VI	MUSEUMS	88

PART II—THE BALTIC

VII	THE YACHT LOST	107
VIII	BALTIC COMMUNITIES	133
IX	A DAY'S SAIL	145

PART III—COPENHAGEN

X	THE DANISH CAPITAL	161
XI	CAFES AND RESTAURANTS	173
XII	ARISTOCRACY AND ART	188
XIII	THE RETURN	198

PART IV—ON THE FRENCH AND FLEMISH COASTS

XIV	FOLKESTONE TO BOULOGNE	211
XV	TO BELGIUM	228
XVI	BRUGES	245

PART V—EAST ANGLIAN ESTUARIES

XVII	EAST ANGLIA	261
XVIII	IN SUFFOLK	280
XIX	THE INCOMPARABLE BLACKWATER	295

LIST OF ILLUSTRATIONS

Aarhus	*Front*
The Embarkation	
By the Quay	
Writing Home	
A Visitor	
A Minor Barge which a Girl will Steer	
The Road is Water in Friesland	
A Friesland Landscape	
At Sneek	
The *Velsa* at Hoorn	
In the Church at Hoorn	
Farmers are Rolling Home	
In the Church at Enkhuisen	
The Klaver Straat, Amsterdam	
At Krasnapolsky's, Amsterdam	
The Café Américain, Amsterdam	
In the Victorian Tea-Room, Amsterdam	
On the Zuyder Zee	
Esbjerg Port	
The Harbor, Esbjerg	
Entering the Baltic	
Gently Sardonic	
The Skipper Shopping	
An Aristocrat Among the Laboring Classes	
The Gate to Sweden	
Consulting the Chart	
Emigrant Girls writing Postal Cards Home	

LIST OF ILLUSTRATIONS

A View from the Bridge, Old Copenhagen	1(
A Copenhagen Café	1(
In the Trivoli Gardens—Amusements during Dinner	1'
A Skipper on a Bicycle	1'
Swedish Exercises on Deck	1!
The Sound—Landing Stage of the Yacht Club	1!
In the Glyptothek—Classic Sculpture and Modern Women	1!
Enjoying the Scenery of the Sound	2!
Early Morn	2!
An Official of the French Republic	2
On the Dunes near Boulogne	2
Making a Diplomatic Episode Out of Nothing at all	2!
A Glimpse of the Kursaal, Ostend	2!
Bathing Tents and Girls	2!
Street Scene in Bruges	2
Scene in Ghent	2
A Rococo Church Interior	2!
A Fish-Restaurant Boat	2
Brightlingsea Creek	2
The Dock, Ipswich	2!
In the Estuary	2
Leaving Maldon	2!
Through the Meadows	3!

PART I
HOLLAND

FROM THE LOG OF THE *VELSA*

CHAPTER I

VOYAGING ON THE CANALS

THE skipper, who, in addition to being a yachtsman, is a Dutchman, smiled with calm assurance as we approached the Dutch frontier in the August evening over the populous water of the canal which leads from Ghent to Terneuzen. He could not abide Belgium, possibly because it is rather like Holland in some ways. In his opinion the bureaucrats of Belgium did not understand yachts and the respect due to them, whereas the bureaucrats of Holland did. Holland was pictured for me as a paradise where a yacht with a seventy-foot mast never had to wait a single moment for a bridge to be swung open. When I inquired about custom-house formalities, I learned that a Dutch custom-house did not exist for a craft flying the sacred blue ensign of the British Naval

FROM THE LOG OF THE *VELSA*

Reserve. And it was so. Merely depositing a ticket and a tip into the long-handled butterfly-net dangled over our deck by the bridge-man as we passed, we sailed straight into Holland, and no word said! But we knew immediately that we were in another country—a country cleaner and neater and more garnished even than Belgium. The Terneuzen Canal, with its brickwork banks and its villages "finished" to the last tile, reminded me of the extravagant, oily perfection of the main tracks of those dandiacal railroads, the North Western in England and the Pennsylvania in America. The stiff sailing breeze was at length favorable. We set the mainsail unexceptionably; and at once, with the falling dusk, the wind fell, and the rain too. We had to depend again on our erratic motor, with all Holland gazing at us. Suddenly the whole canal was lit up on both sides by electricity. We responded with our lights. The exceedingly heavy rain drove me into the saloon to read Dostoyevsky.

At eight P. M. I was dug up out of the depths of Dostoyevsky in order to see my first Dutch harbor. Rain poured through the black night. There was a

VOYAGING ON THE CANALS

plashing of invisible wavelets below, utter darkness above, and a few forlorn lights winking at vast distances. I was informed that we were moored in the yacht-basin of Terneuzen. I remained calm. Had we been moored in the yacht-basin of Kamchatka, the smell of dinner would still have been issuing from the forecastle-hatch, the open page of Dostoyevsky would still have invited me through the saloon skylight, and the amiable ray of the saloon lamp would still have glinted on the piano and on the binnacle with impartial affection. Herein lies an advantage of yachting over motoring. I redescended without a regret, without an apprehension. Already the cook was displacing Dostoyevsky in favor of a white table-cloth and cutlery.

The next morning we were at large on the billows of the West Schelde, a majestic and enraged stream, of which Flushing is the guardian and Antwerp the mistress. The rain had in no wise lost heart. With a contrary wind and a choppy sea, the yacht had a chance to show her qualities and defects. She has both. Built to the order of a Dutch baron rather less than twenty years ago, she

FROM THE LOG OF THE *VELSA*

is flat-bottomed, with lee-boards, and follows closely the lines of certain very picturesque Dutch fishing-smacks. She has a length of just over fifty-five feet and a beam of just over fifteen feet. Her tonnage is fifty-one, except when dues have to be paid, on which serious occasions it mysteriously shrinks to twenty-one net. Yachtsmen are always thus modest. Her rig is, roughly, that of a cutter, with a deliciously curved gaff that is the secret envy of all real cutters.

Her supreme advantage, from my point of view, is that she has well over six feet of head-room in the saloon and in the sleeping-cabins. And, next, that the owner's bed is precisely similar to the celestial bed which he enjoyed on a certain unsurpassed American liner. Further, she carries a piano and an encyclopedia, two necessaries of life. I may say that I have never known another yacht that carried an encyclopedia in more than a score of volumes. Again, she is eternal. She has timbers that recall those of the *Constitution*. There are Dutch eel-boats on the Thames which look almost exactly like her at a distance, and which were launched before Victoria came to the throne. She has a cockpit in

VOYAGING ON THE CANALS

which Hardy might have kissed Nelson. She sails admirably with a moderate wind on the quarter. More important still, by far, she draws only three feet eight inches, and hence can often defy charts, and slide over sands where deep-draft boats would rightly fear to tread; she has even been known to sail through fields.

Possibly for some folk her chief attribute would be that, once seen, she cannot be forgotten. She is a lovely object, and not less unusual than lovely. She is smart also, but nothing more dissimilar to the average smart, conventional English or American yacht can well be conceived. She is a magnet for the curious. When she goes under a railway bridge while a train is going over it, the engine-driver, of no matter what nationality, will invariably risk the lives of all his passengers in order to stare at her until she is out of sight. This I have noticed again and again. The finest compliment her appearance ever received was paid by a schoolboy, who, after staring at her for about a quarter of an hour as she lay at a wharf at Kingston-on-Thames, sidled timidly up to me as I leaned in my best maritime style over the quarter, and asked,

FROM THE LOG OF THE *VELSA*

"Please, sir, is this a training brig?" Romance gleamed in that boy's eye.

As for her defects, I see no reason why I should catalogue them at equal length. But I admit that, to pay for her headroom, she has no promenade-deck for the owner and his friends to "pace," unless they are prepared to exercise themselves on the roof of the saloon. Also that, owing to her shallowness, she will ignobly blow off when put up to the wind. Indeed, the skipper himself, who has proved that she will live in any sea, describes her progress under certain conditions as "one mile ahead and two miles to leeward"; but he would be hurt if he were taken seriously. Her worst fault is due to her long, overhanging prow, which pounds into a head sea with a ruthlessness that would shake the funnels off a torpedo-boat. You must not press her. Leave her to do her best, and she will do it splendidly; but try to bully her, and she will bury her nose and defy you.

That morning on the wide, broad Schelde, with driving rain, and an ever-freshening northwester worrying her bows, she was not pressed, and she did not sink; but her fierce gaiety was such as to keep

BY THE QUAY

VOYAGING ON THE CANALS

us all alive. She threshed the sea. The weather multiplied, until the half-inch wire rope that is the nerve between the wheel and the rudder snapped, and we were at the mercy, etc. While the skipper, with marvelous resource and rapidity, was improvising a new gear, it was discovered amid general horror, that the piano had escaped from its captivity, and was lying across the saloon table. Such an incident counts in the life of an amateur musician. Still, under two hours later, I was playing the same piano again in the tranquillity of Flushing lock.

It was at Middelburg that the leak proved its existence. Middelburg is an architecturally delightful town even in heavy, persevering rain and a northwest gale. It lies on the canal from Flushing to Veere, and its belfry had been a beacon to us nearly all the way down the Schelde from Terneuzen. Every English traveler stares at its renowned town-hall; and indeed the whole place, having been till recently the haunt of more or less honest English racing tipsters and book-makers, must be endeared to the British sporting character. We went forth into the rain and into the town, skirting canals covered with timber-rafts, suffering the lively brutishness of Dutch infants, and gazing at the bare-armed young women under their umbrellas. We also found a goodish restaurant.

When we returned at nine P. M., the deck-hand, a fatalistic philosopher, was pumping. He made a sinister figure in the dark. And there was the sound of the rain on our umbrellas, and the sound of the pumped water pouring off our decks down into the unseen canal. I asked him why he was pumping at that hour. He answered that the ship leaked. It did. The forecastle floor was under an inch of water, and water was pushing up the carpet of the starboard sleeping-cabin, and all the clean linen in the linen-locker was drenched. In a miraculous and terrifying vision, which changed the whole aspect of yachting as a recreation, I saw the yacht at the bottom of the canal. I should not have had this vision had the skipper been aboard; but the skipper was ashore, unfolding the beauties of Holland to the cook. I knew the skipper would explain and cure the leak in an instant. A remarkable man, Dutch only by the accident of birth and parentage, active as a fox-terrier, indefatigable as

VOYAGING ON THE CANALS

a camel, adventurous as Columbus, and as prudent as J. Pierpont Morgan, he had never failed me. Half his life had been spent on that yacht, and the other half on the paternal barge. He had never lived regularly in a house. Consequently he was an expert of the very first order on the behavior of Dutch barges under all conceivable conditions. While the ship deliberately sank and sank, the pumping monotonously continued, and I waited in the saloon for him to come back. Dostoyevsky had no hold on me whatever. The skipper would not come back; he declined utterly to come back; he was lost in the mazy vastness of Middelburg.

Then I heard his voice forward. He had arrived in silence. "I hear our little ship has got a leak, sir," he said when I joined the group of professional mariners on the forward deck, in the thick rain that veiled even gas-lamps. I was disappointed. The skipper was depressed, sentimentally depressed, and he was quite at a loss. Was the leak caused by the buffetings of the Schelde, by the caprices of the piano, by the stress of working through crowded locks? He knew not. But he would swear that the leak was not in the bottom, because the bottom was double. The one thing to do was to go to Veere, and put the ship on a grid that he was aware of in the creek there, and find the leak. And, further, there were a lot of other matters needing immediate attention. The bobstay was all to pieces, both pumps were defective, and the horn for rousing lethargic bridge-men would not have roused a rabbit. All which meant for him an expedition to Flushing, that bustling port!

The ship was pumped dry. But the linen was not dry. I wanted to spread it out in the saloon; but the skipper would not permit such an outrage on the sanctity of the saloon, he would not even let the linen rest in the saloon lavatory (sometimes called the bath-room). It must be hidden like a shame in the forecastle. So the crew retired for the night to the sodden, small forecastle amid soaked linen, while I reposed in dry and comfortable spaciousness, but worried by those sociological considerations which are the mosquitos of a luxurious age—and which ought to be. None but a tyrant convinced of the divine rights of riches could be al-

VOYAGING ON THE CANALS

ways at ease on board a small yacht; on board a large one, as in a house, the contrasts are less point-blank. And yet must small yachts be abolished? Absurd idea! Civilization is not so simple an affair as it seems to politicians perorating before immense audiences.

Owing to the obstinacy of water in finding its own level, we went to bed more than once during that night, and I thought of selling the ship and giving to the poor. What a declension from the glory of the original embarkation!

The next afternoon, through tempests and an eternal downpour, we reached Veere, at the other end of the canal. Veere is full of Scotch history and of beauty; it has a cathedral whose interior is used by children as a field, a gem of a town-hall, and various attractions less striking; but for us it existed simply as a place where there was a grid, to serve the purpose of a dry-dock. On the following morning we got the yacht onto the grid, and then began to wait for the tide to recede. During its interminable recession, we sat under a shed of the shipyard, partly sheltered from the constant rain, and labored to produce abominable water-colors of the yacht, with the quay and the cathedral and the town-hall as a background. And then some one paddling around the yacht in the dinghy perceived a trickle out of a seam. The leak! It was naught but the slight starting of a seam! No trace of other damage. In an hour it had been repaired with oakum and hammers, and covered with a plaster of copper. The steering-gear was repaired. The pumps were repaired. The bobstay was repaired. The water-color looked less abominable in the discreet, kindly light of the saloon. The state of human society seemed less volcanically dangerous. God was in His heaven. "I suppose you 'd like to start early to-morrow morning, sir," said the skipper, whose one desire in life is to go somewhere else. I said I should.

I went ashore with the skipper to pay bills—four gulden for repairs and three gulden for the use of the grid. It would have been much more but for my sagacity in having a Dutch skipper. The charming village proved to be virtually in the possession of one of those formidable English families whose ladies paint in water-colors when no golf-course is near. They ran ecstatically about the

VOYAGING ON THE CANALS

quay with sheets of Whatman until the heavy rain melted them. The owner of the grid lived in a large house with a most picturesque façade. Inside it was all oilcloth, red mahagony, and crimson plush, quite marvelously hideous. The shipwright was an old, jolly man, with white whiskers spreading like a peacock's tail. He gave us cigars to pass the time while he accomplished the calligraphy of a receipt. He was a man sarcastic about his women (of whom he had many), because they would not let him use the *voor-kammer* (front room) to write receipts in. I said women were often the same in England, and he gave a short laugh at England. Nevertheless, he was proud of his women, because out of six daughters five had found husbands, a feat of high skill in that island of Walcheren, where women far outnumber men.

Outside, through the mullioned window, I saw a young matron standing nonchalant and unprotected in the heavy rain. She wore an elaborate local costume, with profuse gilt ornaments. The effect of these Dutch costumes is to suggest that the wearer carries only one bodice, thin and armless, but ten thousand skirts. Near the young matron was a girl of seven or eight, dressed in a fashion precisely similar, spectacle exquisite to regard, but unsatisfactory to think about. Some day all these women will put on long sleeves and deprive themselves of a few underskirts, and all the old, jolly men with spreading white beards will cry out that women are unsexed and that the end of the world is nigh. In another house I bought a fisherman's knitted blue jersey of the finest quality, as being the sole garment capable of keeping me warm in a Dutch summer. I was told that the girl who knitted it received only half a gulden for her labor. Outrageous sweating, which ought never to have been countenanced. Still, I bought the jersey.

At six-thirty next day we were under way—a new ship, as it seemed to me. Yachts may have leaks, but we were under way, and the heavenly smell of bacon was in the saloon; and there had been no poring over time-tables, no tipping of waiters, no rattling over cobbles in omnibuses, no waiting in arctic railway-stations, no pugnacity for corner seats, no checking of baggage. I was wakened by the vibration of the propeller; I clad myself in a toga, and issued forth to laugh good-by at sleeping

WRITING HOME

VOYAGING ON THE CANALS

Veere—no other formalities. And all along the quay, here and there, I observed an open window among the closed ones. Each open window denoted for me an English water-colorist sleeping, even as she or he had rushed about the quay, with an unconcealed conviction of spiritual, moral, and physical superiority. It appeared to me monstrous that these English should be so ill bred as to inflict their insular notions about fresh air on a historic Continental town. Every open window was an arrogant sneer at Dutch civilization, was it not? Surely they could have slept with their windows closed for a few weeks! Or, if not, they might have chosen Amsterdam instead of Veere, and practised their admirable Englishness on the "Victorian Tea-Room" in that city.

We passed into the Veeregat and so into the broad Roompot Channel, and left Veere. It was raining heavily, but gleams near the horizon allowed me to hope that before the day was out I might do another water-color.

CHAPTER II

DUTCH LEISURE

EVERY tourist knows that Holland is one of the historic cradles of political freedom, and also a chain of cities which are in effect museums of invaluable art. The voyager in a little ship may learn that in addition to all this Holland is the home of a vast number of plain persons who are under the necessity of keeping themselves alive seven days a week, and whose experiments in the adventure of living have an interest quite equal to the interest of ancient art. To judge that adventure in its final aspect, one should see Holland on a Sunday, and not the Holland of the cities, but of the little towns.

We came one Sunday morning to a place called Zieriksee, on an island to the north of the East Schelde. Who has heard of Zieriksee? Nevertheless, Zieriksee exists, and seven thousand people prosecute the adventure therein without the aid of

A VISITOR

DUTCH LEISURE

museums and tourists. At first, from the mouth of its private canal, it seems to be a huge, gray tower surrounded by tiniest doll's-houses with vermilion roofs; and as you approach, the tower waxes, until the stones of it appear sufficient to build the whole borough; then it wanes, and is lost in the town, as all towers ultimately are. The cobbled quay and streets were empty as we moored. And in an instant a great crowd sprang up out of the earth,—men and boys and girls, but few women,—staring, glaring, giggling, gabbling, pushing. Their inquisitiveness had no shame, no urbanity. Their cackle deafened. They worried the *Velsa* like starving wolves worrying a deer. The *Velsa* was a godsend, unhoped for, in the enormous and cruel tedium which they had created for themselves. To escape them we forced our way ashore, and trod the clean, deathlike, feet-torturing streets. One shop was open; we entered it, and were supplied with cigarettes by two polite and gracious very old women who knew no English. On emerging from this paganism, we met a long, slow-slouching, gloomy procession of sardonic human beings,—not a pretty woman among them, not a garment that was comely or unclean or unrespectable, not a smile, —the great, faithful congregation marching out of the great church. Here was the life of leisure in Holland as distinguished from the week-day life of industry. It was a tragic spectacle. When we returned to the yacht, the other congregation was still around it. And it was still there, just as noisy and boorish, when we left several hours later. And it would still have been there if we had remained till midnight. The phenomenon of that crowd, wistful in its touching desire for distraction, was a serious criticism of the leaders of men in Holland. As we slid away, we could see the crowd rapidly dissolving into the horror of its original ennui. I asked the cook, a cockney, what he thought of Zieriksee. His face lightened to a cheerful smile.

"Rather a nice sort of place, sir. More like England."

The same afternoon we worked up the Schelde in a dead calm to Zijpe. The rain had pretermitted for the first time, and the sun was hot. Zijpe is a village, a haven, a dike, and a junction of train and steamer. The village lies about a mile inland. The haven was pretty full of barges laid up for

DUTCH LEISURE

Sunday. On the slopes of the haven, near the railway-station and the landing-stage, a multitude of at least a thousand people were strolling to and fro or sitting on the wet grass, all in their formidable Sabbath best. We joined them, in order, if possible, to learn the cause of the concourse; but the mystery remained for one hour and a half in the eventless expanse of the hot afternoon, when the train came in over the flat, green leagues of landscape. We then understood. The whole of Zijpe had turned out to see the afternoon train come in! It was a simple modest Dutch local train, making a deal of noise and dust, and bearing perhaps a score of passengers. But it marked the grand climacteric of leisured existence at Zijpe. We set off to the village, and discovered a village deserted, and a fair-ground, with all its booths and circuses swathed up in gray sheeting. Scarcely a soul! The spirit of romance had pricked them all to the railway-station to see the train come in!

Making a large circuit, we reached again the river and the dike, and learned what a dike is in Holland. From the top of it we could look down the chimneys of houses on the landward side. The population was now on the dike, promenading in magnificent solemnity and self-control. Everybody gravely saluted us in passing. We gravely saluted everybody, and had not a moment to ourselves for miles.

"Over there," said the skipper afterward, pointing vaguely to the southeast over the Schelde, "they 're Roman Catholics. There 's a lot of Spaniards left in Holland." By Spaniards he meant Dutchmen with some Spanish blood.

"Then they enjoy their Sundays?" I suggested.

"Yes," he answered sarcastically, "they enjoy their Sundays. They put their playing-cards in their pockets before they go to church, and then they go straight from the church to the café, and play high, and as like as not knife each other before they 've done." Clearly it takes all sorts to make a little world like Holland, and it is difficult to strike the mean between absolute nullity and homicidal knives. My regret is that the yacht never got as far as those Spaniards gaming and knifing in cafés.

On Monday morning every skipper on every river and canal of Holland tries to prove that the

A MINOR BARGE WHICH A GIRL WILL STEER

DUTCH LEISURE

stagnation of Sunday is only a clever illusion. The East Schelde hummed with express barges at five A. M. It was exactly like a Dutch picture by an old master. Even we, in no hurry, with a strong tide under us and a rising northwester behind us, accomplished fifteen sea-miles in ninety minutes. Craft were taking shelter from the threatened gale. In spite of mistakes by an English crew unaccustomed to a heavy mainsail in tortuous navigation and obstreperous weather, we reached Dordrecht railway bridge without public shame; and then the skipper decided that our engine could not be trusted to push us through the narrow aperture against wind and tide. Hence we bargained with a tug, and were presently attached thereto, waiting for the bridge to open.

Considering that Holland is a country where yachts are understood, and where swing-bridges open at a glance, we had to wait some little time for that bridge; namely, three hours. The patriotism of the skipper was strained. During the whole period the tug rushed to and fro, frisking us wildly about like a kettle at the tail of a busy dog, and continuously collecting other kettles, so that our existence was one long shock and collision. But we saw a good deal of home life on the barges, from a minor barge which a girl will steer to the three-thousand-ton affair that surpasses mail steamers in capacity. There are two homes on these monsters, one at the stem and the other at the stern; the latter is frequently magnificent in spaciousness and gilding. That the two families in the two distant homes are ever intimate is impossible, that they are even acquainted is improbable; but they seem to share a tireless dog, who runs incessantly along the leagues of planking which separate them.

The bridge did at last open, and everything on the river, unmindful of everything else, rushed headlong at the opening, like a crowd of sinners dashing for a suddenly unbarred door into heaven. Our tug jerked us into the throng, a fearful squeeze, and we were through. We cast off, the gulden were collected in a tin, and within five minutes we were moored in the New Haven, under the lee of the Groote Kerk, with trees all around us, in whose high tops a full gale was now blowing.

The next morning our decks were thickly carpeted with green leaves, a singular sight. The har-

DUTCH LEISURE

bor-master came aboard to demand dues, and demanded them in excellent English.

"Where did you learn English?" I asked, and he answered with strange pride:

"Sir, I served seven years under the British flag."

Standing heedless in the cockpit, under driving rain, he recounted the casualties of the night. Fifteen miles higher up the river a fifteen-hundred-ton barge had sunk, and the master and crew, consisting, *inter alia,* of all his family, were drowned. I inquired how such an event could happen in a narrow river amid a numerous population, and learned that in rough weather these barges anchor when a tug can do no more with them, and the crew go to bed and sleep. The water gradually washes in and washes in, until the barge is suddenly and silently engulfed. Dutch phlegm! Corresponding to their Sabbatic phlegm, no doubt. Said the harbor-master:

"Yes, there is a load-line, but they never takes no notice of it in Holland; they just loads them up till they won't hold any more."

The fatalism of the working-classes everywhere

FROM THE LOG OF THE *VELSA*

is perhaps the most utterly astounding of all human phenomena.

Thoughtful, I went off to examine the carved choir-stalls in the Groote Kerk. These choir-stalls are among the most lovely sights in Holland. Their free, fantastic beauty is ravishing and unforgetable; they make you laugh with pleasure as you behold them. I doubt not that they were executed by a rough-tongued man, in a dirty apron, with shocking finger-nails.

THE ROAD IS WATER IN FRIESLAND

CHAPTER III

DUTCH WORK

WE passed through Rotterdam more than once, without seeing more of it than the amazing traffic of its river and its admirable zoölogical gardens full of chromatically inclined parrots; but we stopped at a minor town close by, on a canal off the Meuse, Schiedam. Instinct must have guided me, for the sociological interest of Schiedam was not inconsiderable. Schiedam is called by the Dutch "stinking Schiedam." I made a circuit of the town canals in the dinghy and convinced myself that the epithet was just and not malicious. On the lengthy quays were a large number of very dignified gin distilleries, whose architecture was respectable and sometimes even very good, dating from perhaps early in the last century. Each had a baptismal name, such as "Liverpool," inscribed in large letters across its façade. This rendering decent and this glorification of gin constituted an impressive phenomenon. But it was the provinciality and the uncouth melancholy of the apparently prosperous town that took my fancy. We walked through all its principal streets in the rain, and I thought I had never seen a provinciality so exquisitely painful and perfect. In this city of near thirty thousand people there was not visible one agreeably imposing shop, or one woman attired with intent to charm, or one yard of smooth pavement. I know not why I find an acrid pleasure in thus beholding mediocrity, the average, the everyday ordinary, as it is; but I do. No museum of Amsterdam, The Hague, or Haarlem touched me so nearly as the town of Schiedam, which, after all, I suppose I must have liked.

Toward six o'clock we noticed an unquiet, yet stodgy, gathering in the square where is the electric-tram terminus, then a few uniforms. I asked a superior police officer what there was. He said in careful, tranquil English:

"There is nothing. But there is a strike of glass-workers in the town. Some of them don't want to work, and some of them do want to work. Those

DUTCH WORK

that have worked to-day are being taken home in automobiles. That is all."

I was glad it was all, for from his manner I had expected him to continue to the effect that the glass-workers had been led away by paid agitators and had no good reason to strike. The automobiles began to come along, at intervals, at a tremendous pace, each with a policeman by the chauffeur's side. In one was a single artisan, middle-aged, with a cigar in the corner of his mouth, and a certain adventurous look in his eye. The crowd grimly regarded. The police tried to seem as if they were there by accident, but obviously they lacked histrionic training. In short, the scene was one of the common objects of the wayside of existence all over the civilized world. It presented no novelty whatever, and yet to witness it in Holland was piquant, and caused one to think afresh and perhaps more clearly.

At night, when it had ceased to rain, I was escorting a friend to the station. Musicians were climbing up into the bandstand in the same square. It was Wednesday, the evening of the weekly municipal concert. The railway-station, far out, was superbly gloomy, and it was the only station in Holland where I failed to get a non-Dutch newspaper. The train, with the arrogance of an international express, slid in, slid out, and forgot Schiedam. I emerged from the station alone. A one-horse tram was waiting.

The tram, empty, with a sinking, but everlasting, white horse under a yellow cloth, was without doubt the most provincial and melancholy thing that destiny has yet brought me in contact with. The simple spectacle of it, in the flickering gaslights and in the light of its own lamps, filled the heart, with an anguish inexplicable and beautiful. I got in. An age passed. Then an old workman got in, and saluted; I saluted. Save for the saluting, it was the Five Towns of the eighties over again, intensified, and the last tram out of Hanbridge before the theater-tram.

An age passed. Then a mysterious figure drew the cloth off the horse, and the horse braced up all its four legs. We were starting when a tight-folded umbrella waved in the outer obscurity. An elderly, easy-circumstanced couple arrived upon us with deliberation; the umbrella was a good one.

A FRIESLAND LANDSCAPE

DUTCH WORK

We did start. We rumbled and trundled in long curves of suburban desolation. Then a few miserable shops that ought to have been shut; then the square once more, now jammed in every part with a roaring, barbaric horde. In the distance, over a floor of heads, was an island of illumination, with the figures of puffing and blowing musicians in it; but no rumor of music could reach us through the din. The white horse trotted mildly into and right through the multitude, which jeered angrily, but fell back. An enormous multitude, Gothic, Visigothic, savage, uncivilized, chiefly consisting of young men and big boys—the weekly concert of humanizing music!

I left the tram, and walked along the dark, empty canal-side to the yacht. The impression of stagnation, tedium, provincialism was overwhelming. Nevertheless, here, as in other towns, we were struck by the number of shop-windows with artist's materials for sale. Such was Schiedam. If it is asked whether I went to Holland on a yachting cruise to see this sort of thing, the answer is that I just did.

After a few weeks I began to perceive that Schiedam and similar places, though thrilling, were not the whole of Holland, and perhaps not the most representative of Holland. As the yacht worked northward, Holland seemed to grow more Dutch, until, in the chain of shallow lakes and channels that hold Friesland in a sort of permanent baptism, we came to what was for me the ideal or celestial Holland—everything done by water, even grass cut under water, and black-and-white cows milked in the midst of ponds, and windmills over the eternal flatness used exclusively to shift inconvenient water from one level to another. The road is water in Friesland, and all the world is on the road. If your approach to a town is made perilous by a succession of barges that will obstinately keep the middle of the channel, you know that it is market-day in that town, and the farmers are rolling home in agreeable inebriation.

The motor broke down in Friesland, and we were immobolized in the midst of blue-green fields, red dogs, the cows aforesaid, green milk-floats, blue-bloused sportsmen, and cargoes of cannon-ball cheese. We decided to tow the yacht until we got to a favorable reach. Certain barges sailed past

DUTCH WORK

us right into the eye of the wind, against all physical laws, but the *Velsa* possessed not this magic. We saw three men comfortably towing a string of three huge barges, and we would tow. Unfortunately the only person, the skipper, who knew how to tow had to remain on board. The cook, the deck-hand, and I towed like Greeks pulling against Greeks, and could scarcely move one little yacht. The cook, neurasthenic by temperament, grew sad, until he fell into three feet of inundation, which adventure struck him as profoundly humorous, so that he was contorted with laughter. This did not advance the yacht. Slowly we learned that towing is not mere brute striving, but an art.

We at last came to terms with a tug, as our desire was to sleep at Sneek. Sneek is the veritable metropolis of those regions. After passing, at late dusk, the mysterious night-watchers of eel-nets, who are wakened in their elaborate green-and-yellow boats by a bell, like a Paris concierge, we gradually emerged into nocturnal Sneek through a quadruple lane of barges and tugs so long as to put Sneek among the seven great ports of the world. And even in Sneek at nightfall the impression of immense quantities of water and of greenness, yellowness, and redness was continued. It rained, as usual, in Sneek the next day, but no rain and no water could damp Sneek. It was the most active town any of us had ever seen. It must have been the original "hive of industry." It was full, and full of everything. The market was full of cattle, pigs, and sheep, crowded in pens and in carts; calves, prone, with all four legs tied together, filled acres of pavement. The cafés were full of dealers and drovers, mostly rather jolly, being served by slatternly, pleasant women. The streets were full of good shops, and of boys and girls following us and touching us to see if we existed. (Dreadful little boors!) The barges were full of cauliflowers, cabbages, apples, potatoes, sabots, cheeses, and barrels. The canals were full of barges and steamers.

And immediately one sat down to sketch a group of craft one learned that nothing was stationary. Everything moved that floated—everything on the surface of miles of canal! Everybody, without haste, but without stopping ever, was tirelessly engaged in shifting matter from one spot to another. At intervals a small steamer, twenty, thirty, fifty,

AT SNEEK

DUTCH WORK

eighty tons, would set off for a neighboring village with a few passengers,—including nice girls,—a few cattle, and high piles of miscellaneous packages; or would come in from a neighboring village. The kaleidoscope was everlasting; but it did not fatigue, because it never hurried. Only it made us ashamed of our idleness. Gently occupied old country-women, with head-dresses of lace-work and a gold casque, the whole ridiculously surmounted by a black bonnet for fashion's sake—even these old women made us ashamed of our untransporting idleness.

Having got our engine more or less repaired, we departed from Sneek, a spot that beyond most spots abounds in its own individuality. Sneek is memorable. Impossible to credit that it has fewer than thirteen thousand inhabitants!

As, at breakfast, we dropped down the canal on the way to Leeuwarden, a new guest on board, whose foible is the search for the ideal, and who had been declaiming against the unattractiveness of the women of Munich, spoke thus:

"Is this Dutch bread? I think I should like to become a Dutchman, and live at Sneek, and marry

FROM THE LOG OF THE *VELSA*

a Dutch girl. They have such nice blue eyes, and they 're so calm."

I remarked that I should have thought that his recent experiences in Munich would have frightened him right off the entire sex. He said:

"Well, they 're all beautiful in Vienna, and that worries you just as much in another way. Sneek is the mean."

CHAPTER IV

THE ZUYDER ZEE

WE reached the Zuyder Zee, out of a canal, at Monnikendam, which is a respectably picturesque townlet and the port of embarkation for Marken, the alleged jewel of the Zuyder Zee, the precious isle where the customs and the costumes of a pure age are mingled with the prices of New York for the instruction of tourists. We saw Marken, but only from the mainland, a long, serrated silhouette on the verge. The skipper said that Marken was a side-show and a swindle, and a disgrace to his native country. So I decided to cut it out of the program, and be the owner of the only foreign yacht that had cruised in the Zuyder Zee without visiting Marken. My real reason was undoubtedly that the day's program had been upset by undue lolling in the second-hand shops of Monnikendam. Thus we sailed due north for Hoorn, secretly fearing that at Marken there might be something lovely, unforgetable, that we had missed.

FROM THE LOG OF THE *VELSA*

The Zuyder is a sea agreeable to sail upon, provided you don't mind rain, and provided your craft does not draw more than about six feet. It has the appearance of a sea, but we could generally touch the bottom with our sounding-pole; after all, it is not a sea, but a submerged field. The skipper would tell inclement stories of the Zuyder Zee under ice, and how he had crossed it on foot between Enkhuizen and Stavoren, risking his life for fun; and how he had been obliged to recross it the next day, with more fatigue, as much risk, and far less fun, because there was no other way home. We ourselves knew it only as a ruffled and immense pond, with a bracing atmosphere and the silhouettes of diminished trees and houses sticking up out of its horizons here and there. When these low silhouettes happen to denote your destination, they have the strange faculty of receding from your prow just as fast as you sail toward them, a magic sea of an exquisite monotony; and when you arrive anywhere, you are so surprised at having overtaken the silhouette that your arrival is a dream, in the unreal image of a city.

The one fault of Hoorn is that it is not dead.

THE ZUYDER ZEE

We navigated the Zuyder Zee in order to see dead cities, and never saw one. Hoorn is a delightful vision for the eye—beautiful domestic architecture, beautiful warehouses, beautiful towers, beautiful water-gate, beautiful aniline colors on the surface of dreadful canals. If it were as near to London and Paris as Bruges is, it would be inhabited exclusively by water-colorists. At Hoorn I went mad, and did eight sketches in one day, a record which approaches my highest break at billiards. Actually, it is inhabited by cheese-makers and dealers. No other town, not even Chicago, can possibly contain so many cheeses per head of the population as Hoorn. At Hoorn I saw three men in blue blouses throwing down spherical cheeses in pairs from the second story of a brown and yellow and green warehouse into a yellow cart. One man was in the second story, one in the first, and one in the cart. They were flinging cheeses from hand to hand when we arrived and when we left, and they never dropped a cheese or ceased to fling. They flung into the mysterious night, when the great forms of little cargo-steamers floated soundless over romance to moor at the dark quays, and the long, white English steam-yacht, with its two decks, and its chef and its fluffy chambermaid, and its polished mahogany motor-launch, and its myriad lights and gleams, glided to a berth by the water-tower, and hung there like a cloud beyond the town, keeping me awake half the night while I proved to myself that I did not really envy its owner and that the *Velsa* was really a much better yacht.

The recondite enchantment of Hoorn was intensified by the fact that the English tongue was not current in it. I met only one Dutchman there who spoke it even a little, a military officer. Being on furlough, he was selling cigars in a cigar shop on behalf of his parents. Oh, British army officer! Oh, West Point Academy! He told me that officers of the Dutch army had to be able to speak English, French, and German. Oh, British army officer! Oh, West Point Academy! But he did not understand the phrase "East Indian cigar." He said there were no such cigars in his parents' shop. When I said "Sumatra," he understood, and fetched his mother. When I said that I desired the finest cigars in Hoorn, his mother put away all the samples already exhibited and fetched his

THE ZUYDER ZEE

father. The family had begun to comprehend that a serious customer had strayed into the shop. The father, in apron, with a gesture of solemnity and deference went up-stairs, and returned in majesty with boxes of cigars that were warm to the touch.

"These are the best?"

"These are the best."

I bought. They were threepence apiece.

A mild, deliciously courteous family, recalling the tobacco-selling sisters at Zieriksee, and a pair of tobacconist brothers in the Kalver-Straat, Amsterdam, whose politeness and soft voices would have atoned for a thousand Schiedams. The Dutch middle and upper classes have adorable manners. It was an ordeal to quit the soothing tobacco shop for the terrors of the long, exposed Hoorn High Street, infested, like too many Dutch streets, by wolves and tigers in the outward form of dogs—dogs that will threaten you for a mile and then bite, in order to prove that they are of the race that has always ended by expelling invaders with bloodshed.

I was safer in the yacht's dinghy, on a surface of aniline hues, though the odors were murderous, and though for two hours, while I sketched, three violent young housewives were continually splashing buckets into the canal behind me as they laved and scrubbed every separate stone on the quay. If canals were foul, streets were as clean as table-tops—cleaner.

The other cities of the Zuyder Zee were not more dead than Hoorn, though Enkhuizen, our next port, was more tranquil, possibly because we arrived there on a Saturday evening. Enkhuizen, disappointing at the first glance, exerts a more subtle fascination than Hoorn. However, I remember it as the place where we saw another yacht come in, the owner steering, and foul the piles at the entrance. My skipper looked at *his* owner, as if to say, "You see what owners do when they take charge." I admitted it.

We crossed from Enkhuizen to Stavoren in bad weather, lost the dinghy and recovered it, and nearly lost the yacht, owing to the cook having taken to his bunk without notice when it was imperative to shorten sail in a jiffy. The last that I heard of this cook was that he had become an omnibus conductor. Some people are born to rise, and the born omnibus conductor will reach that es-

IN THE CHURCH AT HOORN

THE ZUYDER ZEE

tate somehow. He was a pleasant, sad young man, and himself painted in water-colors.

I dare say that at Stavoren we were too excited to notice the town; but I know that it was a busy port. Lemmer also was busy, a severely practical town, with a superb harbor-master, and a doctor who cured the cook. We were disappointed with Kampen, a reputed beauty-spot, praised even by E. V. Lucas, who never praises save on extreme provocation. Kampen has architecture,—wonderful gates,—but it also has the cruelest pavements in Holland, and it does not smile hospitably, and the east wind was driving through it, and the rain. The most agreeable corner of Kampen was the charcoal-heated saloon of the yacht. We left Kampen, which perhaps, after all, really was dead, on September 21. The morning was warm and perfect. I had been afloat in various countries for seven weeks continuously, and this was my first warm, sunny morning. In three hours we were at the mouth of the tiny canal leading to Elburg. I was steering.

"Please keep the center of the channel," the skipper enjoined me.

FROM THE LOG OF THE *VELSA*

I did so, but we grounded. The skipper glanced at me as skippers are privileged to glance at owners, but I made him admit that we were within half an inch of the mathematical center of the channel. We got a line on to the pier, and hauled the ship off the sand by brute force. When I had seen Elburg, I was glad that this incident had occurred; for Elburg is the pearl of the Zuyder. Where we, drawing under four feet, grounded at high water in mid-channel, no smart, deep-draft English yacht with chefs and chambermaids can ever venture. And assuredly tourists will not go to Elburg by train. Elburg is safe. Therefore I feel free to mention the town.

Smacks were following one another up the canal for the week-end surcease, and all their long-colored *weins* (vanes) streamed in the wind against the blue sky. And the charm of the inefficient canal was the spreading hay-fields on each side, with big wagons, and fat horses that pricked up their ears (doubtless at the unusual sight of our blue ensign), and a young mother who snatched her rolling infant from the hay and held him up to behold us. And then the skipper was excited by the spectacle of his

THE ZUYDER ZEE

aged father's trading barge, unexpectedly making for the same port, with his mother, brother, and sister on deck—the crew! Arrived in port, we lay under the enormous flank of this barge, and the skipper boarded his old home with becoming placidity.

The port was a magnificent medley of primary colors, and the beautiful forms of boats, and the heavy curves of dark, drying sails, all dominated by the *weins* streaming in the hot sunshine. Every few minutes a smack arrived, and took its appointed place for Sunday. The basin seemed to be always full and always receptive. Nothing lacked for perfect picturesqueness, even to a little ship-repairing yard, and an establishment for raddling sails stretched largely out on green grass. The town was separated from the basin by a narrow canal and a red-brick water-gate. The main street ran straight away inland, and merged into an avenue of yellowish-green trees. At intervals straight streets branched off at right angles from the main. In the center of the burg was a square. Everywhere rich ancient roofs, gables, masonry, and brickwork in Indian reds and slaty-blues; everywhere glimpses of courtyards precisely imitated from the pictures of Pieter de Hooch. The interior of the church was a picture by Bosboom. It had a fine organ-case, and a sacristan out of a late novel by Huysmans. The churchyard was a mass of tall flowers.

The women's costumes here showed a difference, the gilt casque being more visibly divided into two halves. All bodices were black, all skirts blue. Some of the fishermen make majestic figures, tall, proud, commanding, fit adversaries of Alva; in a word, exemplifications of the grand manner. Their salutes were sometimes royal.

The gaiety of the color; the distinction of the forms; the strange warmth; the completeness of the entity of the town, which seemed to have been constructed at one effort; the content of the inhabitants, especially the visible, unconscious gladness of the women at the return of their mariners; the urbanity of everybody—all these things helped to produce a comfortable and yet disconcerting sensation that the old, unreformed world was not quite ripe for utter destruction.

All day until late in the evening smacks ceased not to creep up the canal. The aspect of the basin

FARMERS ARE ROLLING HOME

THE ZUYDER ZEE

altered from minute to minute, with disastrous effect on water-colorists. In the dusk we ferreted in a gloomy and spellbound second-hand shop, amid dozens of rococo wall-clocks, and bought a few little things. As we finally boarded the yacht in the dark, we could see a group of sailors in a bosky arbor bending over a table on which was a lamp that harshly lighted their grave faces. They may have thought that they were calculating and apportioning the week's profits; but in reality they were playing at masterpieces by Rembrandt.

CHAPTER V

SOME TOWNS

HAARLEM is the capital of a province, and has the airs of a minor metropolis. When we moored in the Donkere Spaarne, all the architecture seemed to be saying to us, with innocent pride, that this was the city of the illustrious Frans Hals, and the only place where Frans Hals could be truly appreciated. Haarlem did not stare at strangers, as did other towns. The shops in the narrow, busy Saturday-night streets were small and slow, and it took us most of an evening, in and out of the heavy rain, to buy three shawls, two pairs of white stockings, and some cigarettes; but the shopmen and shop-women, despite their ignorance of English, American, and French, showed no open-mouthed provinciality at our fantastic demands. The impression upon us of the mysterious entity of the town was favorable; we felt at home.

SOME TOWNS

The yacht was just opposite the habitation of a nice middle-class family, and on Sunday morning, through the heavy rain, I could see a boy of sixteen, a girl of fourteen, and a child of five or six, all dressing slowly together in a bedroom that overlooked us, while the father in shirt-sleeves constantly popped to and fro. They were calmly content to see and be seen. Presently father and son, still in shirt-sleeves, appeared on the stoop, each smoking a cigar, and the girl above, arrayed in Sunday white, moved about setting the bedroom in order. It was a pleasant average sight, enhanced by the good architecture of the house, and by a certain metropolitan self-unconsciousness.

We went to church later, or rather into a church, and saw beautiful models of ships hung in the nave, and aged men entering, with their hats on and good cigars in their mouths. For the rest, they resembled superintendents of English Sunday-schools or sidesmen of small parishes. In another church we saw a Sunday-school in full session, a parson in a high pulpit exhorting, secretary and minor officials beneath him, and all the boys standing up with shut eyes and all the girls sitting down with shut eyes. We felt that we were perhaps in the most Protesttant country in Europe.

In the afternoon, when the rain-clouds lifted for a few moments and the museums were closed, we viewed the residential prosperity of Haarlem, of which the chief seat is the Nieuwe Gracht, a broad canal, forbidden to barges, flanked by broad quays beautifully paved in small red brick, and magnificent houses. A feature of the noble architecture here was that the light ornamentation round the front doors was carried up and round the central windows of the first and second stories. A grand street! One properly expected to see elegant women at the windows of these lovely houses,— some were almost palaces,—and one was disappointed. Women there were, for at nearly every splendid window, the family was seated, reading, talking, gazing, or drinking tea; but all the women were dowdy; the majority were middle-aged; none was beautiful or elegant. Nor was any of the visible furniture distinguished.

The beauty of Haarlem seems to be limited to architecture, pavements, and the moral comeliness of

IN THE CHURCH AT ENKHUISEN

SOME TOWNS

being neat and clean. The esthetic sense apparently stops there. Charm must be regarded in Haarlem with suspicion, as a quality dangerous and unrespectable. As daylight failed, the groups within gathered closer and closer to the windows, to catch the last yellow drops of it, and their curiosity about the phenomena of the streets grew more frank. We were examined. In return we examined. And a discussion arose as to whether inspection from within justified inquisitiveness from the street. The decision was that it did not; that a person inside a house had the right to quiz without being quizzed. But this merely academic verdict was not allowed to influence our immediate deportment. In many houses of the lesser streets tables were already laid for supper, and one noticed heavy silver napkin-rings and other silver. In one house the shadowy figures of a family were already grouped round a repast, and beyond them, through another white-curtained window at the back of the spacious room, could be discerned a dim courtyard full of green and yellow foliage. This agreeable picture, typifying all the domestic tranquillity and dignity of prosperous Holland, was the last thing we saw before the dark and the rain fell, and the gas-lamps flickered in.

We entered The Hague through canals pitted by heavy rain, the banks of which showed many suburban residences, undistinguished, but set in the midst of good gardens. And because it was the holiday week,—the week containing the queen's birthday,—and we desired quietude, we obtained permission to lie at the private quay of the gas-works. The creators of The Hague gas-works have made only one mistake: they ought to have accomplished their act much earlier, so that Balzac might have described it; for example, in "The Alkahest," which has the best imaginative descriptions of Dutch life yet written. The Hague gas-works are like a toy, gigantic; but a toy. Impossible to believe that in this vast, clean, scrubbed, swept expanse, where every bit of coal is scrupulously in place, real gas is made. To believe, you must go into the city and see the gas actually burning. Even the immense traveling-cranes, when at work or otherwise, have the air of life-size playthings. Our quay was bordered with flower-beds. The workmen, however, seemed quite real workmen, re-

SOME TOWNS

alistically dirty, who were not playing at work, nor rising at five-thirty A.M. out of mere joyous ecstasy.

Nor did the bargemen who day and night ceaselessly and silently propelled their barges past us into the city by means of poles and sweat, seem to be toying with existence. The procession of these barges never stopped. On the queen's birthday, when our ship was dressed, and the whole town was flagged, it went on, just as the decorated trams and tram-drivers went on. Some of the barges penetrated right through the populous districts, and emerged into the oligarchic quarter of ministries, bureaus, official residences, palaces, parks, art dealers, and shops of expensive lingerie—the quarter, as in every capital, where the precious traditions of correctness, patriotism, red-tape, order, luxury, and the moral grandeur of devising rules for the nice conduct of others are carefully conserved and nourished. This quarter was very well done, and the bargemen, with their perspiring industry, might have had the good taste to keep out of it.

The business center of The Hague, lying between the palaces and the gas-works, is cramped, crowded, and unimpressive. The cafés do not glitter, and everybody knows that the illumination of cafés in a capital is a sure index of a nation's true greatness. Many small cafés, veiled in costly curtains at window and door, showed stray dazzling shafts of bright light, but whether the true greatness of Holland was hidden in these seductive arcana I never knew. Even in the holiday week the principal cafés were emptying soon after ten o'clock. On the other hand, the large stores were still open at that hour, and the shop-girls, whose pale faces made an admirable contrast to their black robes, were still serving ladies therein. At intervals, in the afternoons, one saw a chic woman, moving with a consciousness of her own elegance; but she was very exceptional. The rest might have run over for the day from Haarlem, Delft, Utrecht, or Leyden. In the really excellent and well-frequented music-halls there was no elegance either. I have never anywhere seen better music-hall entertainments than in Holland. In certain major capitals of Europe and elsewhere the public is apt to prove its own essential naïveté by allowing itself to be swindled nightly in gorgeous music-halls. The Dutch are more astute, if less elegant.

THE KALVER-STRAAT, AMSTERDAM

SOME TOWNS

The dying engine of the yacht lost consciousness, for about the twentieth time during this trip, as we were nearing Amsterdam; but a high wind, carrying with it tremendous showers of rain, kindly blew us, under bare poles, up the last half-mile of the North Sea Canal into the private haven of the Royal Dutch Yacht-Club, where we were most amicably received, as, indeed, in all the yacht-club basins of Holland. Baths, telephones, and smoking-rooms were at our disposal without any charge, in addition to the security of the haven, and it was possible to get taxicabs from the somewhat distant city. We demanded a chauffeur who could speak English. They sent us a taxi with two chauffeurs neither of whom could speak any language whatsoever known to philologists. But by the use of maps and a modification of the pictorial writing of the ancient Aztecs, we contrived to be driven almost where we wanted. At the end of the excursion I had made, in my quality of observer, two generalizations: first, that Amsterdam taxis had two drivers for safety; and, second, that taxi-travel in Amsterdam was very exciting and dangerous. But our drivers were so amiable, soft-tongued, and

FROM THE LOG OF THE *VELSA*

energetic that I tipped them both. I then, somehow, learned the truth: one of the men was driving a taxi for the first time, and the other was teaching him.

After driving and walking about Amsterdam for several days, I decided that it would be completely civilized when it was repaved, and not before. It is the paradise of stomachs and the hell of feet. Happily, owing to its canals and its pavements, it has rather fewer of the rash cyclists who menace life in other Dutch cities. In Holland, outside Amsterdam, everybody uses a cycle. If you are run down, as you are, it is just as likely to be by an aged and toothless female peasant as by an office boy. Also there are fewer homicidal dogs in Amsterdam than elsewhere, and there is the same general absence of public monuments which makes other Dutch cities so agreeably strange to the English and American traveler. You can scarcely be afflicted by a grotesque statue of a nonentity in Holland, because there are scarcely any statues.

Amsterdam is a grand city, easily outclassing any other in Holland. Its architecture is distinguished. Its historic past is impressively immanent in the masonry of the city itself, though there is no trace of it in the mild, commonplace demeanor of the inhabitants. Nevertheless, the inhabitants understand solidity, luxury, wealth, and good cheer. Amsterdam has a bourse which is the most peculiar caprice that ever passed through the head of a stock-broker. It is excessively ugly and graceless, but I admire it for being a caprice, and especially for being a stock-broker's caprice. No English stock-broker would have a caprice. Amsterdam has small and dear restaurants of the first order, where a few people with more money than appetite can do themselves very well indeed in hushed privacy. It also has prodigious cafés. Krasnopolshy's—a town, not a café—is said in Amsterdam to be the largest café in Europe. It isn't; but it is large, and wondrously so for a city of only half a million people.

In the prodigious cafés you perceive that Amsterdam possesses the quality which above all others a great city ought to possess. It pullulates. Vast masses of human beings simmer in its thoroughfares and boil over into its public resorts. The narrow Kalver-Straat, even in the rain, is thronged with modest persons who gaze at the superb luxury of its shops. The Kalver-Straat will compete handsomely with Bond Street. Go along the length of it, and you will come out of it thoughtful. Make your way thence to the Rembrandt-Plein, where pleasure concentrates, and you will have to conclude that the whole of Amsterdam is there, and all its habitations empty. The mirrored, scintillating cafés, huge and lofty and golden, are crowded with tables and drinkers and waiters, and dominated by rhapsodic orchestras of women in white who do what they can against the hum of ten thousand conversations, the hoarse calls of waiters, and the clatter of crockery. It is a pandemonium with a certain stolidity. The excellent music-halls and circuses are equally crowded, and curiously, so are the suburban resorts on the rim of the city. Among the larger places, perhaps, the Café Américain, on the Leidsche-Plein, was the least feverish, and this was not to be counted in its favor, because the visitor to a city which pullulates is, and should be, happiest in pullulating. The crowd, the din, the elbowing, the glitter for me, in a town like Amsterdam! In a town like Gouda, which none

AT KRASNAPOLSKY'S, AMSTERDAM

SOME TOWNS

should fail to visit for the incomparable stained-glass in its church, I am content to be as placid and solitary as anybody, and I will follow a dancing bear and a Gipsy girl up and down the streets thereof with as much simplicity as anybody. But Amsterdam is the great, vulgar, inspiring world.

CHAPTER VI

MUSEUMS

I DID not go yachting in Holland in order to visit museums; nevertheless, I saw a few. When it is possible to step off a yacht clean into a museum, and heavy rain is falling, the temptation to remain on board is not sufficiently powerful to keep you out of the museum. At Dordrecht there is a municipal museum manned by four officials. They received us with hope, with enthusiasm, with the most touching gratitude. Their interest in us was pathetic. They were all dying of ennui in those large rooms, where the infection hung in clouds almost visible, and we were a specific stimulant. They seized on us as the morphinomaniac seizes on an unexpected find of the drug.

Just as Haarlem is the city of Frans Hals, so Dordrecht is the city of Ary Scheffer. Posterity in the end is a good judge of painters, if not of heroes, but posterity makes mistakes sometimes,

MUSEUMS

and Ary Scheffer is one of its more glaring mistakes. (Josef Israels seems likely to be another.) And posterity is very slow in acknowledging an error. The Dordrecht museum is waiting for such an acknowledgment. When that comes, the museum will be burned down, or turned into a brewery, and the officials will be delivered from their dreadful daily martyrdom of feigning ecstatic admiration for Ary Scheffer. Only at Dordrecht is it possible to comprehend the full baseness, the exquisite unimportance, of Scheffer's talent. The best thing of his in a museum full of him is a free, brilliant copy of a head by Rembrandt done at the age of eleven. It was, I imagine, his last tolerable work. His worst pictures, solemnly hung here, would be justifiably laughed at in a girls' schoolroom. But his sentimentality, conventionality, and ugliness arouse less laughter than nausea. By chance a few fine pictures have come into the Dordrecht museum, as into most museums. Jakob Maris and Bosboom are refreshing, but even their strong influence cannot disinfect the place nor keep the officials alive. We left the museum in the nick of time, and saw no other visitors.

FROM THE LOG OF THE *VELSA*

Now, the tea-shop into which we next went was far more interesting and esthetically valuable than the museum. The skipper, who knew every shop, buoy, bridge, and shoal in Holland, had indicated this shop to me as a high-class shop for costly teas. It was. I wanted the best tea, and here I got it. The establishment might have survived from the age when Dordrecht was the wealthiest city in Holland. Probably it had so survived. It was full of beautiful utensils in practical daily use. It had an architectural air, and was aware of its own dignity. The head-salesman managed to convey to me that the best tea—that was, tea that a connoisseur would call *tea*—cost two and a half florins a pound. I conveyed to him that I would take two pounds of the same. The head-salesman then displayed to me the tea in its japanned receptacle. He next stood upright and expectant, whereupon an acolyte, in a lovely white apron, silently appeared from the Jan-Steen shadows at the back of the shop, and with solemn gestures held a tun-dish over a paper bag for his superior to pour tea into. Having performed his share in the rite, he disappeared. The parcel was slowly made up, every part of the proc-

THE CAFÉ AMÉRICAIN, AMSTERDAM

MUSEUMS

ess being evidently a matter of secular tradition. I tendered a forty-gulden note. Whereon the merchant himself arrived in majesty at the counter from his office, and offered the change with punctilio. He would have been perfect, but for a hole in the elbow of his black alpaca coat. I regretted this hole. We left the shop stimulated, and were glad to admit that Dordrecht had atoned to us for its museum. Ary Scheffer might have made an excellent tea-dealer.

The museum at Dordrecht only showed in excess an aspect of displayed art which is in some degree common to all museums. For there is no museum which is not a place of desolation. Indeed, I remember to have seen only one collection of pictures, public or private, in which every item was a cause of joy—that of Mr. Widener, near Philadelphia. Perhaps the most wonderful thing in the tourist's Holland is the fact that the small museum at Haarlem, with its prodigious renown, does not disappoint. You enter it with disturbing preliminaries, each visitor having to ring a bell, and the *locus* is antipathetic; but one's pulse is immediately quickened by the verve of those headstrong masterpieces of Hals. And Ruysdael and Jan Steen are influential here, and even the mediocre paintings have often an interest of perversity, as to which naturally the guide-books say naught.

The Teyler Museum at Haarlem also has a few intoxicating works, mixed up with a sinister assortment of mechanical models. And its aged attendant, who watched over his finger-nails as over adored children, had acquired the proper attitude, at once sardonic and benevolent, for a museum of the kind. He was peculiarly in charge of very fine sketches by Rembrandt, of which he managed to exaggerate the value.

Few national museums of art contain a higher percentage of masterpieces than the Mauritshuis at The Hague. And one's first sight of Rembrandt's "Lesson in Anatomy" therein would constitute a dramatic event in any yachting cruise. But my impression of the Mauritshuis was a melancholy one, owing to the hazard of my visit being on the great public holiday of the year, when it was filled with a simple populace, who stared coarsely around, and understood nothing—nothing. True, they gazed in a hypnotized semicircle at "The Lesson in

MUSEUMS

Anatomy," and I can hear amiable persons saying that the greatest art will conquer even the ignorant and the simple. I don't believe it. I believe that if "The Lesson in Anatomy" had been painted by Carolus-Duran, in the manner of Carolus-Duran, the ignorant and the simple would have been hypnotized just the same. And I have known the ignorant and the simple to be overwhelmed with emotion by spurious trickery of the most absurd and offensive kind.

An hour or two in a public museum on a national holiday is a tragic experience, because it forces you to realize that in an artistic sense the majority and backbone of the world have not yet begun to be artistically civilized. Ages must elapse before such civilization can make any appreciable headway. And in the meantime the little hierarchy of art, by which alone art lives and develops, exists precariously in the midst of a vast, dangerous population—a few adventurous whites among indigenous hordes in a painful climate. The indigenous hordes may have splendid qualities, but they have not that one quality which more than any other vivifies. They are jockeyed into paying for the manifestations of art which they cannot enjoy, and this detail is not very agreeable either. A string of fishermen, in their best blue cloth, came into the Mauritshuis out of the rain, and mildly and politely scorned it. Their attitude was unmistakable. They were not intimidated. Well, I like that. I preferred that, for example, to the cant of ten thousand tourists.

Nor was I uplifted by a visit to the Mesdag Museum at The Hague. Mesdag was a second-rate painter with a first-rate reputation, and his taste, as illustrated here, was unworthy of him, even allowing for the fact that many of the pictures were forced upon him as gifts. One or two superb works—a Delacroix, a Dupré, a Rousseau—could not make up for the prevalence of Mesdag, Josef Israels, etc. And yet the place was full of good names. I departed from the museum in a hurry, and, having time to spare, drove to Scheveningen in search of joy. Scheveningen is famous, and is supposed to rival Ostend. It is washed by the same sea, but it does not rival Ostend. It is a yellow and a gloomy spot, with a sky full of kites. Dutchmen ought not to try to rival Ostend. As I

left Scheveningen, my secret melancholy was profoundly established within me, and in that there is something final and splendid. Melancholy when it becomes uncompromisingly sardonic, is as bracing as a bath.

The remarkable thing about the two art museums at Amsterdam, a town of fine architecture, is that they should both—the Ryks and the municipal—be housed in such ugly, imposing buildings. Now, as in the age of Michelangelo, the best architects seldom get the best jobs, and the result is the permanent disfigurement of beautiful cities. Michelangelo often had to sit glum and idle while mediocre architects and artists more skilled than he in pleasing city councils and building-committees muddled away opportunities which he would have glorified; but he did obtain part of a job now and then, subject to it being "improved" by some duffer like Bernini, who of course contrived to leave a large fortune, whereas if Michelangelo had lived to-day he might never have got any job at all.

Incontestably, the exterior, together with much of the interior, of the Ryks depresses. Moreover, the showpiece of the museum, "The Night-Watch" of Rembrandt, is displayed with a too particular self-consciousness on the part of the curator, as though the functionary were saying to you: "Hats off! Speak low! You are in church, and Rembrandt is the god." The truth is that "The Night-Watch" is neither very lovable nor very beautiful. It is an exhibition-picture, meant to hit the wondering centuries in the eye, and it does so. But how long it will continue to do so is a nice question.

Give me the modern side of the Ryks, where there is always plenty of room, despite its sickly Josef Israels. The modern side reëndowed me with youth. It is an unequal collection, and comprises some dreadful mistakes, but at any rate it is being made under the guidance of somebody who is not afraid of his epoch or of being in the wrong. Faced with such a collection, one realizes the shortcomings of London museums and the horror of that steely English official conservatism, at once timid and ruthless, which will never permit itself to discover a foreign artist until the rest of the world has begun to forget him. At the Ryks there are Van Goghs and Cézannes and Bonnards. They are not the best, but they are there. Also there are some of the most superb water-colors of the age, and good things by a dozen classic moderns who are still totally unrepresented in London. I looked at a celestial picture of women—the kind of thing that Guys would have done if he could—painted perhaps fifty years ago, and as modern as the latest Sargent water-color. It was boldly signed T. C. T. C.? T. C.? Who on earth could T. C. be? I summoned an attendant. Thomas Couture, of course! A great artist! He will appear in the National Gallery, Trafalgar Square, about the middle of the twenty-first century.

Then there was Daumier's "Christ and His Disciples," a picture that I would have stolen had it been possible and quite safe to do so. It might seen incredible that any artist of the nineteenth century should take the subject from the great artists of the past, and treat it so as to make you think that it had never been treated before. But Daumier did this. It is true that he was a very great artist indeed. Who that has seen it and understood its tender sarcasm can forget that group of the exalted, mystical Christ talking to semi-incredulous, unperceptive disciples in the gloomy and vague evening landscape? I went back to the yacht and its ignoble and decrepit engine, full of the conviction that art still lives. And I thought of Wilson Steer's "The Music-Room" in the Tate Gallery, London, which magnificent picture is a proof that in London also art still lives.

ON THE ZUYDER ZEE

CHAPTER VII

THE YACHT LOST

OUR adventures toward the Baltic began almost disastrously, because I put into the planning of them too much wisdom and calculation. We had a month of time at our disposal. Now, a fifty-ton yacht in foreign parts thinks nothing of a month. It is capable of using up a month in mere preliminaries. Hence, with admirable forethought, I determined to send the yacht on in advance. The *Velsa* was to cross from her home port, Brightlingsea, to the Dutch coast, and then, sheltered by many islands, to creep along the coasts of Hanover, Holstein, Schleswig, and Denmark, past the mouths of the Elbe, Weser, and Eider, to the port of Esbjerg, where we were to join her by a fast steamer from Harwich. She was then to mount still farther the Danish coast, as far as Liim Fjord and, by a route combining fjords and canals, cross the top of the Jutland peninsula, and enter the desired Baltic by

FROM THE LOG OF THE *VELSA*

Randers Fjord. The banal way would have been through the Kiel Canal. Yachts never take the Liim Fjord; but to me this was a fine reason for taking the Liim Fjord. Moreover, English yachts have a habit of getting into trouble with the German Empire in the Kiel Canal, and English yachtsmen are apt to languish in German prisons on charges of espionage. I was uncertain about the comforts provided for spies in German prisons, and I did not wish to acquire certitude.

So the yacht was despatched. The skipper gave himself the large allowance of a fortnight for the journey to Esbjerg. He had a beautiful new 30-horse-power engine, new sails, a new mast. Nothing could stop him except an east wind. It is notorious that in the North Sea the east wind never blows for more than three days together, and that in July it never blows at all. Still, in this July it did start to blow a few days before the yacht's intended departure. And it continued to blow hard. In a week the skipper had only reached Harwich, a bare twenty miles from Brightlingsea. Then the yacht vanished into the North Sea. The wind held in the east. After another week I learned by ca-

ESBJERG PORT

THE YACHT LOST

ble that my ship had reached the Helder, in North Holland. By a wondrous coincidence, my Dutch skipper's wife and family are established at the Helder. The east wind still held. The skipper spent money daily in saddening me by cable. Then he left the Helder, and the day came for us to board the mail-steamer at Harwich for Esbjerg.

She was a grand steamer, newest and largest of her line. This was her very first trip. She was officered by flaxen, ingenuous, soft-voiced Danes, who had a lot of agreeable Danish friends about them, with whom they chattered in the romantic Danish language, to us exquisite and incomprehensible. Also she was full of original Danish food, and especially of marvelous and mysterious sandwiches, which, with small quantities of champagne, we ate at intervals in a veranda café passably imitated from Atlantic liners. Despite the east wind, which still held, that steamer reached Esbjerg in the twinkling of an eye.

When I say the twinkling of an eye, I mean twenty-two hours. It was in the dusk of a Saturday evening that we had the thrill of entering an unknown foreign country. A dangerous harbor,

FROM THE LOG OF THE *VELSA*

and we penetrated into it as great ships do, with the extreme deliberation of an elephant. There was a vast fleet of small vessels in the basin, and as we slid imperceptibly past the mouth of the basin in the twilight, I scanned the multitudinous masts for the mast of the *Velsa*. Her long Dutch streamer was ever unmistakable. It seemed to us that she ought to be there. What the mail-steamer could do in less than a day she surely ought to have done in more than a fortnight, east wind or no east wind. On the map the distance was simply nothing.

I saw her not. Still, it was growing dark, and my eyes were human eyes, though the eyes of love. The skipper would probably, after all, be on the quay to greet us with his energetic optimism. In fact, he was bound to be on the quay, somewhere in the dark crowd staring up at the great ship, because he never failed. Were miracles necessary, he would have accomplished miracles. But he was not on the quay. The *Velsa* was definitely not at Esbjerg. We felt lonely, forlorn. The head waiter of the Hotel Spangsberg, a man in his way as great as the skipper, singled us out. He had a

THE YACHT LOST

voice that would have soothed the inhabitants of purgatory. He did us good. We were convinced that so long as he consented to be our friend, no serious harm could happen to our universe. And the hotel was excellent, the food was excellent, the cigars were excellent. And the three chambermaids of the hotel, flitting demurely about the long corridor at their nightly tasks, fair, clad in prints, foreign, separated romantically from us by the palisades of language—the three modest chambermaids were all young and beautiful, with astounding complexions.

The next morning the wind was north by east, which was still worse than east or northeast for the progress of the yacht toward us. Nevertheless, I more than once walked down across the wharves of the port to the extreme end of the jetty—about a mile each way each time—in the hope of descrying the *Velsa's* long, red streamer in the offing. It was Sunday. The town of Esbjerg, whose interest for the stranger is strictly modern and sociological, was not attractive. Its main street, though extremely creditable to a small town, and a rare lesson to towns of the same size in England, was not a thoroughfare in which to linger, especially on Sunday. In the entire town we saw not a single beautiful or even ancient building. Further, the port was asleep, and the strong, gusty breeze positively offensive in the deceptive sunshine.

We should have been bored, we might even have been distressed, had we not gradually perceived, in one passing figure after another, that the standard of female beauty in Esbjerg was far higher than in any other place we had ever seen. These women and girls, in their light Sunday summer frocks, had beauty, fine complexions, grace, softness, to a degree really unusual; and in transparent sleeves or in no sleeves at all they wandered amiably in that northerly gale as though it had been a southern zephyr. We saw that our overcoats were an inelegance, but we retained them. And we saw that life in Esbjerg must have profound compensations. There were two types of beautiful women, one with straight lips, and the other with the upper lip like the traditional bow. The latter, of course, was the more generously formed, acquiescent and yet pouting, more blonde than the blonde. Both types had the effect of making the foreigner feel that to be

THE HARBOR, ESBJERG

THE YACHT LOST

a foreigner and a stranger in Esbjerg, forcibly aloof from all the daily frequentations and intimacies of the social organism, was a mistake.

In the afternoon we hired an automobile, ostensibly to inspect the peninsula, but in fact partly to see whether similar women prevailed throughout the peninsula, and partly to give the yacht a chance of creeping in during our absence. In our hearts we knew that so long as we stood looking for it it would never arrive. In a few moments, as it seemed, we had crossed the peninsula to Veile, a sympathetic watering-place on its own fjord, and were gazing at the desired Baltic, whereon our yacht ought to have been floating, but was not. It seemed a heavenly sea, as blue as the Mediterranean.

We had driven fast along rather bad and dusty roads, and had passed about ten thousand one-story farmsteads, brick-built, splendidly thatched, and each bearing its date on the walls in large iron figures. These farmsteads, all much alike, showed that some great change, probably for the better, must have transformed Danish agriculture about thirty or forty years ago. But though farmers were driving abroad in two-horse vehicles, and though certain old men strolled to and fro, smoking magnificent pipes at least a foot and a half long, the weight of which had to be supported with the hand, there was little evidence of opulence or even of ease.

The passage of the automobile caused real alarm among male cyclists and other wayfarers, who, in the most absurd, girlish manner, would even leap across ditches to escape the risks of it. The women, curiously, showed much more valor. The dogs were of a reckless audacity. From every farmyard, at the sound of our coming, a fierce dog would rush out to attack us, with no conception of our speed. Impossible to avoid these torpedoes! We killed one instantaneously, and ran over another, which somersaulted, and, aghast, then balanced itself on three legs. Scores of dogs were saved by scores of miracles. Occasionally we came across a wise dog that must have had previous altercations with automobiles, and learned the lesson. By dusk we had thoroughly familiarized ourselves with the flat Danish landscape, whose bare earth is of a rich gray purple; and as we approached Esbjerg again,

THE YACHT LOST

after a tour of 120 miles, we felt that we knew Jutland by heart, and that the yacht could not fail to be waiting for us in some cranny of the port, ready to take us to other shores. But the yacht had not come.

Then the head waiter grew to be our uncle, our father, our consoler. It is true that he told us stories of ships that had set forth and never been heard of again; but his moral influence was invaluable. He soothed us, fed us, diverted us, interpreted us, and despatched cables for us. We called him "Ober," a name unsuitable to his diminutive form, his few years, and his chubby face. Yet he was a true Ober. He expressed himself in four languages, and could accomplish everything. In response to all our requests, he would murmur in his exquisitely soft voice, "Oh, yes! oh, yes!" He devised our daily excursions. He sent us to Ribe, the one ancient town that we saw on the peninsula, in the cathedral of which was a young girl who had stepped out of a picture by Memling, and who sold post-cards with the gestures of a virgin saint and the astuteness of a dealer. He sent us to the island of Fanö, where the northeaster blows straight from

FROM THE LOG OF THE *VELSA*

Greenland across a ten-mile bathing-beach peopled by fragile women who saunter in muslin in front of vast hotels beneath a canopy of flags that stand out horizontally in the terrible breeze. He provided us with water-bottles and with plates (for palettes), so that we could descend to the multicolored port, and there, half sheltered from the wind by a pile of fish-boxes and from the showers by an umbrella, produce wet water-colors of fishing-smacks continually in motion.

Day followed day. We had lived at Esbjerg all our lives. The yacht was lost at sea. The yacht had never existed. The wife of the skipper, or, rather, his widow, had twice cabled that she had no news. But the Ober continued to bear our misfortunes with the most astounding gallantry. And then there came a cable from the skipper, dated from the island of Wangeroog. . . . Wangeroog! Wangeroog! What a name for an impossible island! What a name for an island at which to be weatherbound! We knew it not. Baedeker knew it not. Even the Ober had not heard of it. We found it at last on a map more than a hundred miles to the south. And I had been walking

ENTERING THE BALTIC

THE YACHT LOST

down to the jetty thrice a day to gaze forth for the *Velsa's wein!*

The skipper in his cable asked us to meet him at Friedrichstadt, on the Eider, in Holstein, Germany. The trains were very slow and awkward. The Ober said:

"Why do you not take an automobile? Much quicker."

"Yes; but the German customs?"

"Everything shall be arranged," said the Ober.

I said:

"I don't see myself among the German bureaucracy in a hired car."

The Ober said calmly:

"I will go with you."

"All the way?"

"I will go with you all the way. I will arrange everything. I speak German very well. Nothing will go wrong."

Such a head waiter deserved encouragement. I encouraged him. He put on his best clothes, and came, smoking cigars. He took us faultlessly through the German customs at the frontier. He superintended our first meal at a small German hotel. I asked him to join us at table. He bowed and accepted. When the meal was over, he rose and bowed again. It was a good meal. He took us through three tire-bursts amid the horrid wastes of Schleswig-Holstein. He escorted us into Friedrichstadt, and secured rooms for us at the hotel. Then he said he must return. No! no! We could not let him abandon us in the harsh monotony of that excessively tedious provincial town. But he murmured that he must depart. The yacht might not arrive for days yet. I shuddered.

"At any rate," I said, "before you leave, inquire where the haven is, and take me to it, so that I may know how to find it."

He complied. It was a small haven; a steamer and several ships were in it. Behind one ship I saw a mast and a red pennant somewhat in the style of the *Velsa*.

"There," I said, "my yacht has a mast rather like that."

I looked again. Utterly impossible that the *Velsa* could have arrived so quickly; but it was the *Velsa*. Joy! Almost tears of joy! I led the Ober on board. He said solemnly:

THE YACHT LOST

"It is very beautiful."

So it was.

But our things were at the hotel. We had our rooms engaged at the hotel.

The Ober said:

"I will arrange everything."

In a quarter of an hour our baggage was on board, and there was no hotel bill. And then the Ober really did depart, with sorrow. Never shall I look on his like again. The next day we voyaged up the Eider, a featureless stream whose life has been destroyed by the Kiel Canal, to its junction with the Kiel Canal, eighty-six dull, placid kilometers. But no matter the dullness; we were afloat and in motion.

We spent about seventy-two hours in the German Empire, and emerged from it, at Kiel, by the canal, with a certain relief; for the yacht had several times groaned in the formidable clutch of the Fatherland's bureaucracy. She had been stopped by telephone at Friedrichstadt for having passed the custom-house at the mouth of the Eider, the said custom-house not being distinguished, as it ought to have been, by the regulation flag. Again we were stopped by telephone at Rendsburg, on the canal, for having dared to ascend the Eider without a pilot. Here the skipper absolutely declined to pay the pilot-fees, and our papers were confiscated, and we were informed that the panjandrum of the harbor would call on us. However, he did not call on us; he returned our papers, and let us go, thus supporting the skipper's hotly held theory that by the law of nations yachts on rivers are free.

We were obliged to take a pilot for the canal. He was a nice, companionable man, unhealthy, and gently sardonic. He told us that the canal would be remunerative if war-ships paid dues. "Only they don't," he added. Confronted with the proposition that the canal was very ugly indeed, he repudiated it. He went up and down the canal forever and ever, and saw nothing but the ships on it and the navigation signals. He said that he had been piloting for twelve years, and had not yet had the same ship twice. And there were 150 pilots on the canal!

We put him ashore and into the arms of his wife at Kiel, in heavy rain and the customary northeaster, and we pushed forward into the comparative

GENTLY SARDONIC

freedom of Kiel Fjord, making for Friedrichsort, which looked attractive on the chart. But Friedrichsort was too naval for us; it made us feel like spies. We crossed hastily to Möltenort, a little pleasure town. Even here we had not walked a mile on land before we were involved in forts and menacing sign-boards. We retreated. The whole fjord was covered with battle-ships, destroyers, submarines, Hydro-aëroplanes curved in the atmosphere, or skimmed the froth off the waves. The air was noisy with the whizzing of varied screws. It was enormous, terrific, intimidating, especially when at dusk search-lights began to dart among the lights of the innumerable fjord passenger-steamers. We knew that we were deeply involved in the tremendous German system. Still, our blue ensign flew proudly, unchallenged.

The population of Möltenort was not seductive, though a few young men here and there seemed efficient, smart, and decent. The women and girls left us utterly unmoved. The major part of the visitors were content to sit vacantly on the promenade at a spot where a powerful drain, discharging into the fjord, announced itself flagrantly to the

FROM THE LOG OF THE *VELSA*

sense. These quiet, tired, submissive persons struck us as being the raw slavish material of the magnificent imperial system, and entirely unconnected with the wondrous brains that organized it and kept it going. The next morning we departed very early, but huge targets were being towed out in advance of us, and we effected our final escape into the free Baltic only by braving a fleet of battleships that fired into the checkered sky. Sometimes their shells glinted high up in the sun, and seemed to be curving along the top edge of an imaginary rainbow. We slowly left them astern, with, as I say, a certain relief. Little, unmilitary Denmark lay ahead.

THE SKIPPER SHOPPING

CHAPTER VIII

BALTIC COMMUNITIES

AT Vordingborg, a small town at the extreme south of Sjælland, the largest and easternmost of the Danish islands, we felt ourselves to be really for the first time in pure and simple Denmark (Esbjerg had a certain international quality). We had sailed through the Langelands Belt, skirting the monotonous agricultural coasts of all sorts of islands, great and small, until one evening we reached this city, which looked imposing on the map. When we had followed the skipper ashore on his marketing expedition, and trodden all the stony streets of little Vordingborg, we seemed to know what essential Denmark, dozing in the midst of the Baltic, truly was.

Except a huge and antique fort, there was no visible historical basis to this town. The main thoroughfare showed none of the dignity of tradition. It was a bourgeois thoroughfare, and comfortable bourgeoises were placidly shopping therein—the same little bourgeoises that one sees all over the world. A fairly large hotel; sundry tobacconists; a bookseller who also sold wall-papers; a sausage-shop, with a girl actuating an efficient sausage-slicing machine, and in the window an electric fan whirring close to a gigantic sausage. In the market, on a vague open space, a few carts, with their shafts on the ground; a few stalls; a few women; a butcher whipping off a hungry dog; three cheeses on a stand; baskets of fruit and vegetables on the Danish ground; our skipper chattering by signs and monosyllables in the middle. That was Vordingborg.

In the churchyard there were only two graves. The church had no more architectural interest than a modern church in a London suburb, though it was older. We went within. The numbers of the hymns at the last service were still forlornly stuck up on the indicator. The altar and screen were ingenuously decorated in the style of a high-class booth at a fair. Three women in huge disfiguring aprons were cleaning the interior. Their cloaks and a white umbrella lay on the stone floor. They never even glanced at us. We left the church, and then skirting market-gardens and climbing over the ramparts of the fort, we descended to the mournful little railway station, and as we watched a little train amble plaintively in and out of that terminus, we thought of the numbers of the hymns sung at the last service in the church, and the immense devastating ennui of provincial existence in remote places enveloped us like a dank fog. We set sail, and quitted Vordingborg forever, lest we might harden our hearts and be unjust to Vordingborg, which, after all, at bottom, must be very like a million other townlets on earth.

Compared with some of the ports we made, Vordingborg was a metropolis and a center of art. When we had threaded through the Ulfsund and the Stege Strand and the intricacies of the Rogesträmmen, we found shelter in a village harbor of the name of Faxo. Faxo had nothing—nothing but a thousand trucks of marl, a girl looking out of a window, and a locked railway station. We walked inland into a forest, and encountered the railway track in the middle of the forest, and we walked back to Faxo, and it was the same Faxo, except that a splendid brig previously at anchor in the outer roads was slipping away in the twilight, and leaving us alone in Faxo.

At Spotsbjerg, on the north of the island of Sjælland, a small, untidy fishing village with a harbor as big as a swimming-bath, there was not even a visible church; we looked vainly for any church. But there was a telephone, and on the quay there was a young and pretty girl leaning motionless on her father's, or her grandfather's, tarpaulin shoulder. Full of the thought that she would one day be old and plain, we fled from Spotsbjerg, and traveled an incredible distance during the whole of a bright Sunday, in order to refresh our mundane instincts at the capital of the Jutland peninsula, Aarhus.

And on approaching Aarhus, we ran into a regatta, and the *Velsa* had less of the air of an aristocrat among the industrial classes than in such ports as Spotsbjerg and Faxo. Further, a reporter came to obtain a "story" about the strange Dutch yacht with the English ensign. It was almost equal to being anchored off the Battery, New York.

ARISTOCRAT AMONG THE LABORING CLASSES

BALTIC COMMUNITIES

At Aarhus the pulse of the world was beating rather loud. In the windows of the booksellers' shops were photographs of the director of the municipal theater surrounded by his troupe of stars. And he exactly resembled his important brethren in the West End of London. I myself was among the authors performed in the municipal theater, and I had a strange, comic sensation of being world-renowned. Crowds surged in the streets of Aarhus and in its cafés and tram-cars, and at least one of its taxicabs was driven by a woman. It had a really admirable hotel, the Royal, with first-class cooking, and a concert every night in its winter garden, where the ruling classes met for inexpensive amusement, and succeeded in amusing themselves with a dignity, a simplicity, and a politeness that could not possibly be achieved in any provincial town in England, were it five times the size of Aarhus. And why?

Withal, Aarhus, I have to confess, was not much of a place for elegance. Its women failed, and the appearance of the women is the true test of a civilization. So far in our Danish experience the women of Esbjerg stood unrivaled. The ladies of Aarhus, even the leading ladies gathered together in the Royal Hotel, lacked style and beauty. Many of them had had the sense to retain the national short sleeve against the ruling of fashion, but they did not arrive at any effect of individuality. They were neither one thing nor the other. Their faces showed kindness, efficiency, constancy, perhaps all the virtues; but they could not capture the stranger's interest.

There was more style at Helsingör (Elsinore), a town much smaller than Aarhus, but probably enlivened by naval and military influences, by its close proximity to Sweden, with train-ferry communication therewith, and by its connection with Hamlet and Shakspere. The night ferries keep the town unduly awake, but they energize it. Till a late hour the station and the quay are busy with dim figures of chattering youth in pale costumes, and the departure of the glittering train-laden ferry to a foreign country two miles off is a romantic spectacle. The churches of Helsingör have an architectural interest, and its fruit shops display exotic fruits at high prices. Officers flit to and fro on bicycles. Generals get out of a closed cab at the railway station, and they bear a furled standard, and vanish importantly with it into the arcana of the station. The newspapers of many countries are for sale at the kiosk. The harbor-master is a great man, and a suave.

The pride of Helsingör is the Kronborg Castle, within sight of the town and most grandiosely overlooking sea and land. Feudal castles are often well placed, but one seldom sees a renaissance building of such heroic proportions in such a dramatically conceived situation. The castle is of course used chiefly as a barracks. On entering the enormous precincts, we saw through a window a private sitting on a chair on a table, in fatigue uniform, playing mildly a flageolet, and by his side on the table another private in fatigue uniform, with a boot in one hand, doing nothing whatever. And from these two figures, from the whitewashed bareness of the chamber, and from the flageolet, was exhaled all the monstrous melancholy of barrack-life, the same throughout the world.

Part of the castle is set aside as a museum, wherein, under the direction of a guide, one is permitted to see a collection of pictures the surpassing ugliness of which nearly renders them interesting. The guide points through a window in the wall ten feet thick to a little plot of turf. "Where Hamlet walked." No historical authority is offered to the visitor for this statement. The guide then leads one through a series of large rooms, empty save for an occasional arm-chair, to the true heart of the Kronborg, where he displayed to us a seated statue of Mr. Hall Caine, tinted an extreme unpleasant bluish-white. An inscription told that it had been presented to Kronborg by a committee of Englishmen a few years earlier to mark some anniversary. The guide said it was a statue of Shakspere. I could not believe him.

THE GATE TO SWEDEN

CHAPTER IX

A DAY'S SAIL

ALTHOUGH there is a lively pleasure in discovering even the dullest and smallest towns and villages, the finest experience offered by the Baltic is the savor of the Baltic itself in a long day's sail. I mean a day of fourteen hours at least, from six in the morning till eight at night, through varied seascapes and landscapes and varied weather. As soon as the yacht leaves harbor in the bracing chill of sunrise she becomes a distinct entity, independent, self-reliant. The half-dozen men on her, cut off from the world, are closely knitted into a new companionship, the sense of which is expressed not in words, but by the subtleties of tone and mien; and if only one among them falls short of absolute loyalty and good-will toward the rest, the republic is a failure, and the air of ocean poisoned. The dictum of an older and far more practised yachtsman than myself used al-

FROM THE LOG OF THE *VELSA*

ways to be, "I'll have no man aboard my ship who can't smile all the time." It is a good saying. And it could be applied to my yacht in the Baltic. We had days at sea in the Baltic which were ideal and thrilling from one end to the other.

To make a final study of the chart in the cabin while waiting for breakfast is a thrilling act. You choose a name on the chart, and decide: "We will go to that name." It is a name. It is not yet a town or a village. It is just what you imagine it to be until you first sight it, when it instantly falsifies every fancy. The course is settled. The ship is on that course. The landmarks will suffice for an hour or two, but the sea-marks must be deciphered on the chart, which is an English chart, and hence inferior in fullness and clearness to either French or Dutch charts. Strange, this, for a nation preëminently maritime! To compensate, the English "Sailing Directions"—for example, the "Pilot's Guide to the Baltic"—are so admirably written that it is a pleasure to read them. Lucid, succinct, elegant, they might serve as models to a novelist. And they are anonymous.

To pick up the first buoy is thrilling. We are

THE CHART

A DAY'S SAIL

all equally ignorant of these waters; the skipper himself has not previously sailed them, and we are all, save the cook, engulfed below amid swaying saucepans, on the lookout for that buoy. It ought to be visible at a certain hour, but it is not. The skipper points with his hand and says the buoy must be about there, but it is not. He looks through my glasses, and I look through his; no result. Then the deck-hand, without glasses, cries grinning that he has located her. After a quarter of an hour I can see the thing myself. That a buoy? It is naught but a pole with a slightly swollen head. Absurd to call it a buoy! Nevertheless, we are relieved, and in a superior manner we reconcile ourselves to the Baltic idiosyncrasy of employing broom-handles for buoys. The reason for this dangerous idiosyncrasy neither the skipper nor anybody else could divine. Presently we have the broom close abeam, a bobbing stick all alone in the immense wilderness of water. There it is on the chart, and there it is in the water, a romantic miracle. We assuage its solitude for a few minutes, and then abandon it to loneliness.

We resume the study of the chart; for although

FROM THE LOG OF THE *VELSA*

we are quite sure of our course, the skipper can never be sure enough. My attention is drawn to a foot-note that explains the ice-signals of the Baltic. And the skipper sets to telling tales of terror about the ice, in the Zuyder Zee and other seas. He tells how the ice forms under the ship surreptitiously, coming up from the bottom like treacle. You say, "It's freezing to-night," and the next morning the ship can't move; and you may die of starvation, for though the ice will hold the ship, it won't hold you. The skipper knew men who could remember ice in the Zuyder Zee in June. He himself had once oscillated for a whole week between two ports on the Zuyder Zee, visible to each other, pushed hither and thither by the ice, and unable to get anywhere at all. But ice was less terrible than it used to be, owing to the increased strength and efficiency of ice-breakers. And climate was less rigorous. Thus the skipper would reassure us for a moment, only to intimidate us afresh. For it seems that the ice has a way of climbing; it will climb up over everything, and inclose a ship. Indeed, he was most impressive on the subject of ice. He said that the twin horrors

A DAY'S SAIL

of the sea were ice and fog. But of fog he told no tales, being occupied with the forward valve of the engine. We perceived that yachtsmen who go out when it happens to suit them, between May and September only, can never achieve intimacy with the entire individuality of the sea.

The weather has now cleared for a while. The sun is hot, the saloon skylight warm to the touch. You throw off a jersey. The tumbling water is a scale of deep blues, splendid against the brass of the bollard and the reddishness of the spars. The engine is running without a "knock"; the sails are nicely filled; the patent log is twirling aft. A small rainbow shines steadily in the foam thrown up from the bows, and a great rainbow stretches across all heaven, with its own ghost parallel to it. Among the large, soft clouds rags of dark cloud are uneasily floating. On the flat shores of near islands the same cereals ripen as ripen at home. And this is thrilling. Distant islands are miraged. Even a distant battleship seems to be lifted clean out of the water by the so-called mirage.

And then a trading-schooner, small, but much larger than us, relentlessly overhauls us. She laughs at the efforts of our engine to aid our sails, and forges ahead, all slanting, with her dinghy slung up tight aft, over her rudder. And then it is the still small voice of the stomach that speaks. Hunger and repletion follow each other very swiftly on such days. The after-breakfast cigar is scarcely finished before a genuine curiosity as to the menu of lunch comes to birth within. We glance into the saloon. Yes, the white cloth is laid, but we cannot eat cloth. The cook and the chronometer are conspiring together against us.

In the afternoon the weather is thick and squally. And we are creeping between sad and forlorn veiled islands that seem to exude all the melancholy of the seas. There is plenty of water, but only in a deceiving horizontal sense. The channel is almost as narrow and as tortuous as a Devonshire lane. English charts are criminally preposterous, and so are Danish brooms. Hardly can one distinguish between a starboard and a port broom. Is the life of a yacht to depend on such negligent devices? The skipper is worried. And the spectacle of a ship aground in mid-sea does not tranquilize. Sometimes the hail wipes out for a few

EMIGRANT GIRLS WRITING POSTAL CARDS HOME

A DAY'S SAIL

seconds the whole prospect. The eyes of everybody are strained with looking for distant brooms.

Then we are free of the archipelago, and also the sky clears. The sun, turning orange, is behind us, and the wind in our teeth. Ahead is a schooner, beating. And she is the schooner of the morning. Our engine now has the better of her. As we overtake her, she runs away on one tack, and comes back on the next. She bears down on our stern, huge, black, glittering. A man and a boy are all her crew. This man and this boy are entitled to be called mariners, as distinguished from yachtsmen. We can see their faces plainly as they gaze down at us from their high deck. And you may see just the same faces on the liners that carry emigrants from Denmark to the West, and the same limbs sprawling on the decks of the Esbjerg steamers, as the same hands scrawl Danish characters on picture postal cards to the inhabitants of these very islands.

The sea is now purple, and the schooner a little black blot on the red panorama of the sunset; and ahead, amid faint yellow and green fields, is a white speck, together with sundry red specks and blue specks. The name on the chart! And then the haven is descried, and a ring of masts with fluttering rags. And then the lighthouse and the roofs detach themselves, and the actual mouth of the haven appears. Twilight falls; the engine is moderated; the deck-hand stands by with a pole. Very slowly we slide in, and the multitudinous bright tints of the fishing-smacks are startlingly gay even in the dusk. The skipper glances rapidly about him, and yells out in Dutch to a fisherman, who replies in Danish. The skipper shakes his head, at a loss, and gives an order to the deck-hand. The deck-hand claws with a pole at a yellow smack. We have ceased to be independent. The name on the chart is a name no longer. It is a living burg, a poor little place, good enough to sleep in, and no more. But another stage on the journey to that magic capital Copenhagen.

A VIEW FROM THE BRIDGE—OLD COPENHAGEN

CHAPTER X

THE DANISH CAPITAL

ACROSS the great expanse of Kjöge Bay, Copenhagen first became visible as a group of factory chimneys under a firmament of smoke. We approached it rapidly upon smooth water, and ran into the narrowing bottle-neck of Kallebo, with the main island of Sjælland to the west and the appendant island of Amager to the east. Copenhagen stands on both, straddling over a wide connecting bridge which carries double lines of electric trams and all the traffic of a metropolis. When a yacht, even a small one, wishes to enter the harbor, this bridge is cut in two and lifted into the air, and the traffic impatiently champs its bit while waiting for the yacht.

Apparently they understand yachts at Copenhagen, as they do in Holland. At the outer barrier of the harbor we were not even requested to stop. A cheerful and beneficent functionary cried out for our name, our captain's name, our tonnage, and our immediate origin, and, his curiosity being sated, waved us onward. The great bridge bisected itself for us with singular promptitude. Nevertheless, the gold-buttoned man in charge thereof from his high perch signaled to us that our burgee was too small. We therefore, having nothing else handy to placate him, ran up a blue ensign to the masthead; but it looked so excessively odd there, so acutely contrary to the English etiquette of yachts, that we at once hauled it down again. No further complaint was made.

We were now in the haven, and over the funnels of many ships we could see the city. It was all copper domes and roofs; and we saw that it was a proud city, and a city where exposed copper turns to a beautiful green instead of to black, as in London. Splendid copper domes are the chief symptom of Copenhagen. After all the monotonous, tiny provincialism of the peninsula and of the islands, it was sensational to find a vast capital at the far end of the farthest island. We thought we were coming to the end of the world, and we came to a complete and dazzling city that sur-

THE DANISH CAPITAL

passed, for example, Brussels in its imposingness. We turned westward out of the main channel into the heart of the town, and in a moment were tied up to a smack, and the red-and-green bourse was leaning over us; the rattle and ringing and stamping of horses, lorries, tram-cars, and taxi-cabs deafened us on three sides; and a bridge trembling with traffic barred our way.

Towers and spires rose beyond the bridge; crowds stood to gaze at us; steamers and warehouses filled the prospect to the north; and under our bows the petrol-engined gondolas of Copenhagen, each holding a dozen passengers or so, continually shot. We were in the midst of a terrific din, but we cared not. We had arrived, and we had arrived in a grand town; we knew that at the first glance.

In something less than half an hour one of us had gone forth and returned with grave tidings: "This is a most exciting city. I've already seen lots of beautiful women, some with lovely tow-colored hair." The charm of distant Esbjerg was at last renewed. I went forth myself, into a very clean, fresh-looking city, with simple and lively inhabitants. In a trice I had gazed at the Thorvaldsen Museum (which I had no intention of entering, Thorvaldsen being for me on about the same artistic plane as the inexcusable Ary Scheffer of Dordrecht), the Christianborg Palace, which had an austere and kingly air, the very modern and admirable town hall, the old railway station, which has been transformed into the largest kinema in the world, the floating fish shops and fish restaurants (made out of old smacks and schooners), the narrow, thronged shopping streets, the celebrated Tivoli establishment, and the yacht-like steamers that from a quay, which might almost be called the gate to Sweden, in the very middle of the town, are constantly setting sail for Scandinavia. From Copenhagen you go to Sweden as thoughtlessly as in New York you go from Forty-second to Sixty-ninth Street, or in London from the Bank to Chelsea, and with less discipline. If the steamer has cast off, and the captain sees you hurrying up the street, he stops his engines and waits for you, and you are dragged on board by a sailor; whereupon the liner departs, unless the captain happens to see somebody else hurrying up the street.

A COPENHAGEN CAFÉ

THE DANISH CAPITAL

An hour in the thoroughfares of Copenhagen was enough to convince my feet that it was not a city specially designed for pedestrians. I limped back to the yacht, and sent the skipper to hire a carriage. He knew no more of the city than I did, less indeed; he could no more than I speak a single word of Danish; but I felt sure that he would return with an equipage. What I desired was an equipage with a driver who could speak either English, French, or Dutch. He did return with an equipage, and it was overpowering. Rather like a second-hand state carriage, it was drawn by two large gray horses, perhaps out of a circus, and driven by a liveried being who was alleged to speak French. I shuddered at the probable cost of this prodigious conveyance, but pretended I did not care. The figure named was just seven dollars a day. We monopolized the carriage during our sojourn, and the days were long; but the coachman never complained. Possibly because he had no language in which to complain. We learned in a moment that his ability to speak French was entirely mythical. Then some one said that a misunderstanding had occurred at the livery-stables, and that German was the foreign language he spoke. But he did not speak German either, nor anything else. He was just another of those strange creatures met in the course of travel who are born, who mature, and who die without speaking or comprehending any language whatever.

From the height of his spacious and sedate vehicle we gazed down upon the rushing population of Copenhagen—beautiful women, with lovely tow-colored hair, and simple, nice-gestured men. The driver only made one mistake, but it was a bad one. We wanted tea, and we asked him to go to a tea-garden, any tea-garden. He smiled, and went. He took us up an interminable boulevard, with a special strip for cyclists. Thousands upon thousands of cyclists, all fair, passed and repassed us. He went on and on. One of the horses fell lame, but it made no difference. We could not stop him. And repetitions of the word for tea in French and German had no effect save to make him smile. We constantly descried what seemed in the distance to be tea-gardens, but they were not tea-gardens. We saw an incomprehensible colony of doll's-

THE DANISH CAPITAL

houses—well-kept suburban huts exteriorly resembling houses—in a doll's garden. We could not conceive the nature of this phenomenon, but it was not a tea-garden. Presently the carriage was stopped by a man demanding money. He wore no uniform, but conveyed to us that he was an official of the town of Hillerup, and that strange carriages had to pay forty-eight öre in order to traverse Hillerup. It seemed a lot of money; but as it only amounted to sixpence, we paid. The man may have been a highwayman. We looked at the map for Hillerup, and found it miles away from Copenhagen.

We were now in serious need of tea, and helpless. The driver drove on. He conducted us through half a dozen seaside resorts on the quite unjustly celebrated "Danish Riviera"; he came actually to the end of the tram-line, and then he curved inland into a forest (more to pay). We were now angry and still helpless. The forest had no end, and the roads in it no direction. Desperate, we signaled to him to turn back. He would not. He informed us on his fingers that he would be arriving in twenty minutes or so. When he did arrive, we solved the mystery. He had confused the word for tea with the word for deer, and had brought us to a well-known country resort called the Deer Park. A few miserable tourists were in fact drinking cold, bad tea on a windy terrace overlooking a distant horizon, far beyond which lay Copenhagen. We swallowed the tea, the driver swallowed beer, and we started back. We had no overcoats, and the Baltic evening was cold. Trams overtook us flying at a tremendous pace into Copenhagen, and we were behind a lame horse. In the dusk we reached once more the desirable city, whose women never seemed more fair to us than they did then. This adventure taught us that the yachtsman must be prepared for any adventure, even the wildest.

IN THE TIVOLI GARDENS—AMUSEMENTS DURING DINNER

CHAPTER XI

CAFÉS AND RESTAURANTS

THE most interesting thing, to the complete stranger, in a large foreign city that does not live on its own past is not the museums, but the restaurants and cafés, even in the dead season. We were told that August was the dead season in Copenhagen, and that all the world was at the seaside resorts. We had, however, visited a number of Danish seaside resorts, and they were without exception far more dead than Copenhagen. In particular Marienlyst, reputed to be the haunt of fashion and elegance, proved to be a very sad, deserted strand. Copenhagen was not dead.

We went for our first dinner to Wivels Restaurant, signalized to us by authority as the finest in Denmark, a large, rambling, crimson-and-gold place, full of waiters who had learned English in America, of hors-d'œuvre, and of music. The band was much better than the food, but it has to be said that we arrived at half-past seven, when Danish dinner is over and Danish supper not begun. Still, many middle-class people were unceremoniously and expensively eating—in the main hors-d'œuvre. The metropolitanism of Copenhagen was at once apparent in this great restaurant. The people had little style, but they had the assurance and the incuriousness of metropolitans, and they were accustomed to throwing money about, and to glare, and to stridency, and to the idiosyncrasies of waiters, and to being in the swim. Wivels might show itself on Fifth Avenue or in the Strand without blushing. And its food had the wholesale, crude quality of the food offered in these renowned streets to persons in the swim.

Next we went to the Hôtel d'Angleterre, which was just the restaurant of the standardized international hotel. Once within its walls, and you might as well be at Paris, Aix-les-Bains, Harrogate, Rome, Algiers, Brussels, as at Copenhagen. The same menu, the same cooking, the same waiters, the same furniture, the same toothpicks, and the same detestable, self-restrained English travelers, with their excruciating Englishness. The café

CAFÉS AND RESTAURANTS

on the ground floor of this hotel, overlooking a large and busy circular *place,* with the opera and other necessaries of metropolitan life close by, was more amusing than the restaurant. It was a genuine resort in the afternoon. The existence of Copenhagen rolled to and fro in front of its canopied terrace, and one might sit next to an English yachting party of astounding correctness and complacency (from one of those conceited three-hundred-ton boats, enameled white, and jeweled in many holes, like a watch), or to a couple of Danish commercials, or to a dandy and his love. Here we one night singled out for observation a very characteristic Danish young man and young woman with the complexions, the quiet, persuasive voices, and the soothing gestures of the North. It was an agreeable sight; but when we had carried our observation somewhat further, we discovered that they were an English pair on their honeymoon.

In a day or two, feeling more expert in things Danish, we wanted a truly Danish restaurant, unspoiled by cosmopolitanism. We hit on it in the Wiener Café, appanage of the Hotel King of Denmark. A long, narrow room, anciently and curiously furnished, with mid-Victorian engravings on the somber walls. The waiters had the austerity of priests presiding at a rite. Their silent countenances said impassively: "This is the most select resort in our great and historic country. It has been frequented by the flower of Danish aristocracy, art, and letters for a thousand years. It has not changed. It never will. No upstart cosmopolitanism can enter here. Submit yourselves. Speak in hushed tones. Conform to all the niceties of our ceremonial, for we have consented to receive you."

In brief, it was rather like an English bank, or a historic hotel in an English cathedral town, though its food was better, I admit. The menu was in strict Danish. We understood naught of it, but it had the air of a saga. At the close of the repast, the waiter told us that, for the *prix fixe,* we had the choice between cake and cheese. I said, "Will you let me have a look at the cake, and then I'll decide." He replied that he could not; that the cake could not be produced unless it was definitively ordered. The strange thing was that he

A SKIPPER ON A BICYCLE

CAFÉS AND RESTAURANTS

persisted in this attitude. Cake never had been shown on approval at the Wiener Café of the Hotel King of Denmark, and it never would be. I bowed the head before an august tradition, and ordered cheese. The Wiener Café ought to open a branch in London; it was the most English affair I have ever encountered out of England.

Indeed, Copenhagen is often exquisitely English. That very night we chose the restaurant of the Hotel —— for dinner. The room was darkly gorgeous, silent, and nearly full. We were curtly shown to an empty table, and a menu was flung at us. The head waiter and three inefficient under waiters then totally ignored us and our signals for fifteen minutes; they had their habitués to serve. At the end of fifteen minutes we softly and apologetically rose and departed, without causing any apparent regret save perhaps to the hat-and-coat boy, whom we basely omitted to tip.

We roved in the wet, busy Sunday streets, searching hungrily for a restaurant that seemed receptive, that seemed assimilative, and luck guided us into the Café de l'Industrie, near the Tivoli. The managers of this industrious café had that peculiar air, both independent and amicable, which sits so well on the directors of an organism that is firmly established in the good-will of the flourishing mass. No selectness, no tradition, no formality, no fashion, no preposterous manners about the Café de l'Industrie, but an aspect of solid, rather vulgar, all-embracing, all-forgiving prosperity. It was not cheap, neither was it dear. It was gaudy, but not too gaudy. The waiters were men of the world, experienced in human nature, occupied, hasty, both curt and expansive, not servile, not autocratic. Their faces said: "Look here, I know the difficulties of running a popular restaurant, and you know them, too. This is not heaven, especially on a Sunday night; but we do our best, and you get value for your money."

The customers were samples of all Copenhagen. They had money to spend, but not too much. There were limits to their recklessness in the pursuit of joy. They were fairly noisy, quite without affectation, fundamentally decent, the average Danish. Elegance was rarer than beauty, and spirituality than common sense, in that restaurant. We ate moderately in the din and clash of hors-d'œuvre, mural decorations, mirrors, and music, and thanked our destiny that we had had the superlative courage to leave the Hotel ——, with its extreme correctitude.

Finally, among our excursions in restaurants, must be mentioned a crazy hour in the restaurant of the Hotel ——, supreme example of what the enterprising spirit of modern Denmark can accomplish when it sets about to imitate the German *art nouveau*. The —— is a grand hotel in which everything, with the most marvelous and terrifying ingenuity, has been designed in defiance of artistic tradition. A fork at the —— resembles no other fork on earth, and obviously the designer's first and last thought was to be unique. It did not matter to him what kind of fork he produced so long as it was different from any previous fork in human history. The same with the table-cloth, the flower-vase, the mustard-pot, the chair, the carpet, the dado, the frieze, the tessellated pavement, the stair-rail, the wash-basin, the bedstead, the quilt, the very door-knobs. The proprietors of the place had ordered a new hotel in the extreme sense, and their order had been fulfilled. It was a prodigious undertaking, and must certainly have been costly. It was impressive proof of real initiative. It intimidated the beholder, who had the illusion of being on another planet. Its ultimate effect was to outrival all other collections of ugliness. I doubt whether in Berlin itself such ingenious and complete ugliness could be equaled in the same cubic space. My idea is that the creators of the Hotel —— may lawfully boast of standing alone on a pinnacle.

It was an inspiration on the part of the creators, when the hotel was finished to the last salt-spoon, to order a number of large and particularly bad copies of old masters, in inexpensive gilt frames, and to hang them higgledy-piggledy on the walls. The resulting effect of grotesquery is overwhelming. Nevertheless, the —— justly ranks as one of the leading European hotels. It is a mercy that the architect and the other designers were forbidden to meddle with the cooking, which sins not by any originality.

The summary and summit of the restaurants and cafés of Copenhagen is the Tivoli. New York has nothing like the Tivoli, and the Londoner can

SWEDISH EXERCISES ON DECK

CAFÉS AND RESTAURANTS

only say with regret that the Tivoli is what Earl's Court ought to be, and is not. The Tivoli comprises, within the compass of a garden in the midst of the city, restaurants, cafés, theater, concert-hall, outdoor theater, bands, pantomime, vaudeville, dancing-halls, and very numerous side-shows on both land and water. The strangest combinations of pleasure are possible at the Tivoli. You can, for instance, as we did, eat a French dinner while watching a performance of monkeys on a tight-rope. The opportunities for weirdness in felicity are endless. We happened to arrive at Copenhagen just in time for the fêtes celebrating the seventieth anniversary of the Tivoli, which is as ancient as it is modern. On the great night the Tivoli reveled until morning. It must be the pride of the populace of Copenhagen, and one of the city's dominating institutions. It cannot be ignored. It probably uses more electric light than any other ten institutions put together. And however keenly you may resent its commonplace attraction, that attraction will one day magnetize you to enter its gates—at the usual fee.

I estimate that I have seen twenty thousand peo-

FROM THE LOG OF THE *VELSA*

ple at once in the Tivoli, not a bad total for one resort in a town of only half a million inhabitants. And the twenty thousand were a pleasant sight to the foreign observer, not merely for the pervading beauty and grace of the women, which was remarkable, but also for the evident fact that as a race the Danish know how to enjoy themselves with gaiety, dignity, and simplicity. Their demeanor was a lesson to Anglo-Saxons, who have yet to discover how to enjoy themselves freely without being either ridiculous or vulgar or brutish. The twenty thousand represented in chief the unassuming middle-class of Copenhagen.

There were no doubt millionaires, aristocrats, "nuts," rascals, odalisks, and mere artisans among the lot, but the solid bulk was the middle-class, getting value for its money in an agreeable and unexceptionable manner. The memory of those thousands wandering lightly clad in the cold Northern night, under domes and festoons and pillars of electric light, amid the altercations of conflicting orchestras, or dancing in vast, stuffy inclosures, or drinking and laughing and eating hors-d'œuvre under rustling trees, or submitting gracefully to

CAFÉS AND RESTAURANTS

Wagnerian overtures in a theater whose glazed aisles were two restaurants, or floating on icy lakes, or just beatifically sitting on al-fresco seats in couples—this memory remains important in the yachtsman's experiences of the Baltic.

CHAPTER XII

ARISTOCRACY AND ART

THE harbor-master would not allow us to remain for more than three days in our original berth, which served us very well as a sort of grand stand for viewing the life of Copenhagen. His theory was that we were in the way of honest laboring folk, and that we ought to be up in the "sound," on the northeastern edge of the city, where the yachts lie. We contested his theory, but we went, because it is unwise to quarrel with a bureaucracy of whose language you are ignorant.

The sound did not suit us. The anchorage was opposite a coaling station, and also opposite a shipbuilding yard, and from the west came a strong odor out of a manufactory of something unpleasant. We could have tolerated the dust, the noise, and the smell, but what we could not tolerate was the heavy rolling, for the north wind was blowing and the anchorage exposed to it. Indeed, the

ARISTOCRACY AND ART

Royal Danish Yacht Club might have chosen more comfortable quarters for itself. We therefore unostentatiously weighed anchor again, and reëntered the town, and hid ourselves among many businesslike tugs in a little creek called the New Haven, whose extremity was conveniently close to the Café d'Angleterre. We hoped that the prowling harbor-master would not catch sight of us, and he did not.

The aristocratic and governing quarter of the town lay about us, including the Bregade, a street full of antiquaries, marble churches, and baroque houses, and the Amalienborg Palace, which is really four separate similar palaces (in an octagonal *place*) thrown into one. Here all the prospects and vistas were dignified, magnificent, and proudly exclusive. The eighteenth century had nobly survived, when the populace was honestly regarded as a horde created by divine providence in order that the ruling classes might practise upon it the art of ruling. There was no Tivoli when those beautiful pavements were made, and as you stand on those pavements and gaze around at the royal grandiosity, speckless and complete, you can almost imagine that even the French Revolution has not yet occurred. The tiny, colored sentry at the vast, gray gates is still living in the eighteenth century. The architecture is not very distinguished, but it has style. It shames the —— Hotel. The Frederiks Church, whose copper dome overtops the other copper domes, is a fair example of the quarter. Without being in the least a masterpiece, it imposes by its sincerity and its sense of its own importance. And the interior is kept as scrupulously as a boudoir. The impeccability of the marble flooring is wondrous, and each of the crimson cushions in the polished pews is like a lady's pillow. Nothing rude can invade this marmoreal fane.

The Rosenborg Palace, not far off, is open to the public, so that all may judge what was the life of sovereigns in a small country, and what probably still is. The royal villas outside Florence are very ugly, but there is a light grace about their furnishing which lifts them far above the heavy, stuffy, tasteless mediocrity of such homes as the Rosenborg. Badly planned, dark, unhygienic, crammed with the miscellaneous ugliness of generations of royal buying, the Rosenborg is rather a sad sight to people of taste; and the few very lovely things that have slipped in here and there by inadvertence only intensify its mournfulness. The phantoms of stupid courtiers seem to pervade, strictly according to etiquette, its gloomy salons. And yet occasionally, in the disposition of an arm-chair or a screen, one realizes that it must, after all, have been a home, inhabited by human beings worthy of sympathy. It is the most bourgeois home I ever entered. In a glass case, with certain uniforms, were hung the modern overcoat (a little frayed) and the hat of a late monarch. They touched the heart of the sardonic visitor, their exposure was so naïve.

Even more depressing than this mausoleum of nineteenth-century manners was the museum of art. As a colossal negation of art, this institution ranks with the museum of Lausanne. It is an enormous and ugly building, full of enormous ugliness in painting and sculpture. It contained a fine Rembrandt—"Christ at Emmaus"—and one good modern picture, a plowing scene by Wilhelmson. We carefully searched the immense rooms for another good modern picture, and found it not. Even the specimens of Gauguin, Van Gogh, and Bonnard were mediocre.

The sculpture was simply indescribable. The eye roamed like a bird over the waters of the deluge, and saw absolutely nothing upon which to alight with safety. Utter desolation reigned. The directors of this museum had never, save in the case of Wilhelmson, been guilty of an inadvertence. Their instinct against beauty in any form was unerring. Imagine the stony desert of rooms and corridors and giant staircases on a wet Sunday morning, echoing to the footsteps of the simple holiday crowd engaged patriotically in the admiration of Danish art; imagine ingenuous, mackintoshed figures against the vast flanks of stiff and terrific marble Venuses and other gods; imagine the whispering in front of anecdotes in paint; imagine the Inferno of an artist—and you have the art museum, the abode and lurking-place of everlasting tedium.

Quite different is the Glyptothek, a museum whose existence is due to private enterprise and munificence. It is housed in an ugly and ill-planned building, but the contents are beautiful,

IN THE GLYPTOTHEK—CLASSIC SCULPTURE AND MODERN WOMEN

ARISTOCRACY AND ART

very well arranged, and admirably exposed. The Glyptothek has an entrancing small picture by Tiepolo, of Antony and Cleopatra meeting, which I was informed must be a study for a larger picture in Venice. It alone should raise the museum to a shrine of pilgrimage, and it is not even mentioned in Baedeker! But the Glyptothek triumphs chiefly by its sculpture. Apart from its classical side, it has a superb collection of Meuniers, which impressed, without greatly pleasing, me; a roomful of Rodin busts which are so honest and lifelike and jolly that when you look at them you want to laugh —you must laugh from joy. And the Carpeaux busts of beautiful women—what a profound and tranquil satisfaction in gazing at them!

Some of the rooms at the Glyptothek are magical in their effect on the sensibility. They would make you forget wife and children, yachts, income tax, and even the Monroe Doctrine. Living Danish women were apposite enough to wander about the sculpture rooms for our delectation, making delicious contrasts against the background of marble groups.

CHAPTER XIII

THE RETURN

WE left Copenhagen with regrets, for the entity of the town was very romantic and attractive. Even the humble New Haven, where we sheltered from the eye of the harbor-master, had its charm for us. It was the real sailors' quarter, thoroughly ungentlemanly and downright. The shops on each side of the creek were below the level of the street and even of the water, and every one of them was either a café, with mysterious music beating behind glazed doors, or an emporium of some sort for sailors. Revelries began in the afternoon. You might see a nice neat Danish wife guiding an obstreperously intoxicated Danish sailor down the steps leading to a cigar shop. Not a pleasant situation for a nice wife! But, then, you reflected that he was a sailor, and that he had doubtless been sober and agreeable a short while before, and would soon be sober and

THE RETURN

agreeable again; and that perhaps there were great compensations in his character. At night Bacchus and Pan were the true gods of that quarter, and the worship of them was loud and yet harmonious.

We prepared reluctantly to depart; the engine also. The engine would not depart, and it was a new engine. Two hours were spent in wheedling and conciliating its magneto. After that the boat traveled faster than it had ever traveled. We passed out of Copenhagen into the sound, leaving a noble array of yachts behind, and so up the sound. Soon Copenhagen was naught but a bouquet of copper domes, and its beautiful women became legendary with us, and our memory heightened their beauty. And then the engine developed a "knock." Now, in a small internal-conbustion engine a "knock" may be due to bad petrol or to a misplacement of the magneto or to a hundred other schisms in the secret economy of the affair. We slowed to half-speed and sought eagerly the origin of the "knock," which, however, remained inexplicable. We were engloomed; we were in despair.

We had just decided to stop the engine when it stopped of itself, with a fearful crash of broken metal. One side of the casing was shattered. The skipper's smile was tragical. The manliness of all of us trembled under the severity of the ordeal which fate had administered. To open out the engine-box and glance at the wreck in the depths thereof was heart-rending. We could not closely examine the chaos of steel and brass because it was too hot, but we knew that the irremediable had occurred in the bowels of the *Velsa*. We made sail, and crawled back to the sound, and mournfully anchored with our unseen woe among the other yachts.

The engine was duly inspected bit by bit; and it appeared that only the bearing of the forward piston was broken, certainly owing to careless mounting of the engine in the shops. It was an enormous catastrophe, but perhaps not irremediable. Indeed, within a short time the skipper was calculating that he could get a new bearing made in Copenhagen in twenty-four hours. Anyhow, we had to reconcile ourselves to a second visit to Copenhagen. And Copenhagen, a few hours earlier so sweet a name in our ears, was now hateful to us, a kind of purgatory to which we were condemned for the sins of others.

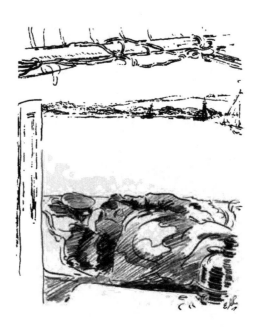

ENJOYING THE SCENERY OF THE SOUND

THE RETURN

The making and fitting of the new bearing occupied just seventy hours. During this interminable period we enjoyed the scenery of the sound and grew acquainted with its diverse phenomena. The weather, if wet, was calm, and the surface of the water smooth; but every steamer that passed would set up a roll that flung books, if not crockery, about the saloon. And the procession of steamers in both directions was constant from five A. M. to midnight. They came from and went to every part of the archipelago and of Sweden and of northern Germany. We gradually understood that at Copenhagen railways are a trifle, and the sea a matter of the highest importance. Nearly all traffic is seaborne.

We discovered, too, that the immediate shore of the sound, and of the yacht-basin scooped out of it, was a sort of toy seaside resort for the city. Part of the building in which the Royal Danish Yacht Club is housed was used as a public restaurant, with a fine terrace that commanded the yacht-club landing-stage and all the traffic of the sound. Moreover, it was a good restaurant, except that the waiters seemed to be always eating some titbit on the sly.

FROM THE LOG OF THE *VELSA*

Here we sat and watched the business and pleasure of the sound. The czar's yacht came to anchor, huge and old-fashioned and ungraceful, with a blue-and-white standard large enough to make a suit of sails for a schooner—the biggest yacht afloat, I think, but not a pleasing object, though better than the antique ship of the Danish king. The unwieldy ceremoniousness of Russian courts seemed to surround this pompous vessel, and the solitary tragedy of imperial existence was made manifest in her. Ah, the savage and hollow futility of saluting guns! The two English royal yachts, both of which we saw in the neighborhood, were in every way strikingly superior to the Russian.

Impossible to tire of the spectacle offered by that restaurant terrace. At night the steamers would slip down out of Copenhagen one after the other to the ends of the Baltic, and each was a moving parterre of electricity on the darkness. And then we would walk along the nocturnal shore and find it peopled with couples and larger groups, whose bicycles were often stacked in groups, too. And the little yachts in the little yacht-basin were each an illuminated household! A woman would emerge from a cabin and ask a question of a man on the dark bank, and he would flash a lantern-light in her face like a missile, and "Oh!" she would cry. And farther on the great hulk which is the home of the Copenhagen Amateur Sailing Club would be lit with festoons of lamps, and from within it would come the sounds of song and the laughter of two sexes. And then we would yell, "*Velsa,* ahoy!" and keep on yelling until all the lightly clad couples were drawn out of the chilly night like moths by the strange English signaling. And at last the *Velsa* would wake up, and the dinghy would detach itself from her side, and we would go aboard. But not until two o'clock or so would the hilarity and music of the Amateur Sailing Club cease, and merge into a frantic whistling for taxicabs from the stand beyond the restaurant.

Then a few hours' slumber, broken by nightmares of the impossibility of ever quitting Copenhagen, and we would get up and gaze at the sadness of the dismantled engine, and over the water at the yachts dozing and rocking in the dawn. And on a near yacht, out of the maw of a forecastle-hatch left open for air, a half-dressed sailor would appear, and yawn, and stretch his arms, and then begin to use a bucket on the yacht's deck. The day was born. A green tug would hurry northward, splashing; and the first of the morning steamers would arrive from some mystical distant island, a vessel, like most of the rest, of about six hundred tons, red and black funnels, the captain looking down at us from the bridge; a nice handful of passengers, including a few young women in bright hats; everything damp and fresh, and everybody expectant and braced for Copenhagen. A cheerful, ordinary sight! And then our skipper would emerge, and the cook with my morning apple on a white plate. And the skipper would say, "We ought to be able to make a start to-day, sir." And on the third day we did make a start, the engine having been miraculously recreated; and we left Copenhagen, hating it no more.

EARLY MORN

PART IV
ON THE FRENCH AND FLEMISH COAST

CHAPTER XIV

FOLKESTONE TO BOULOGNE

WE waited for the weather a day and a night at Folkestone, which, though one of the gateways of England, is a poor and primitive place to lie in. Most of the time we were on the mud, and to get up into England we had to climb a craggy precipice called the quay-wall. Nevertheless, the harbor (so styled) is picturesque, and in the less respectable part of the town, between the big hotels and band-stands and the mail-steamers; there are agreeable second-hand book shops, in one of which I bought an early edition of Gray's poems bound in ancient vellum.

The newspapers were very pessimistic about the weather, and smacks occasionally crept in for shelter, with wild reports of what was going on in the channel. At four o'clock in the morning, however, we started, adventurous, for the far coasts of Brittany, via Boulogne. The channel was a gray and desolate sight, weary and uneasy after the gale. And I also was weary and uneasy, for it is impossible for a civilized person of regular habits to arise at four A. M. without both physical and psychical suffering, and the pleasure derived from the experience, though real, is perverse. The last gleams of the Gris-Nez and the Varne lights were visible across the heaving waste, feebly illuminating the intense melancholy of the dawn. There was nothing to do except steer and keep your eyes open, because a favorable and moderate southwest wind rendered the engine unnecessary. The ship, and the dinghy after her, pitched and rolled over the heavy swell. The skipper said naught. I said naught. The lights expired. The dark gray of the sea turned to steel. The breeze was icy. Vitality was at its lowest. Brittany seemed exceedingly remote, even unattainable. Great, vital questions presented themselves to the enfeebled mind, cutting at the very root of all conduct and all ambitions. What was the use of yachting? What was the use of anything? Why struggle? Why exist? The universe was too vast, and the soul homeless therein.

AN OFFICIAL OF THE FRENCH REPUBLIC

FOLKESTONE TO BOULOGNE

And then the cook, imperfectly attired, came aft, bearing a brass tray, and on the tray an electro-teapot, sugar-basin, and milk-jug, and a white cup and saucer with a spoon. Magic paraphernalia! Exquisite and potent draft, far surpassing champagne drunk amid the bright glances of beauty! Only the finest China tea is employed aboard the *Velsa*. I drank, and was healed; and I gave also to the skipper. Earth was transformed. We began to talk. The wind freshened. The ship, heeling over, spurted. It was a grand life. We descried the French coast. The hours flew. Before breakfast-time we were becalmed, in sunshine, between the piers at Boulogne, and had to go in on the engine. At 8:15 we ran her on the mud, on a rising tide, next to a pilot-boat, the *Jean et Marie,* inhabited by three jolly French sailors. We carried a warp to the Quai Chanzy, and another to a buoy, and considered ourselves fairly in France.

The officials of the French republic on the quay had been driven by the spectacle of our peculiar Dutch lines and rig to adopt strange, emotional attitudes; and as soon as we were afloat, the French republic came aboard in a dinghy manned by two acolytes. The skipper usually receives the representatives of foreign powers, but as the skipper speaks no French, and as this was the first time I had entered France in this style, I thought I would be my own ambassador. I received the French republic in my saloon; we were ravishingly polite to each other; we murmured sweet compliments to each other. He gave me a clean bill of health, and went off with four francs and one half-penny. There is no nation like the French. A French milliner will make a hat out of a piece of felt and nothing; and a French official will make a diplomatic episode out of nothing at all, putting into five minutes of futility all the Gallic civilization of centuries.

Boulogne Harbor is a very bustling spot, and as its area is narrowly limited, and its entrance difficult, the amount of signaling that goes on is extraordinary. A single ship will fill the entrance; hence a flag flies to warn the surrounding seas when the entrance is occupied or about to be occupied. The state of the tide is also indicated, and the expert can read from hieroglyphics slung in the air the exact depth of water at a particular moment be-

FOLKESTONE TO BOULOGNE

tween the piers. In addition, of course, there is the weather signaling. We had scarcely been in port a couple of hours before the weather signaling shocked us; nay, we took it as an affront to ourselves. The south cone went up. We had come in at the tail-end of one south gale, and now another was predicted! How could small people like us hope to work our way down to Brittany in the teeth of the gale! And I had an appointment in the harbor of Carantec, a tiny village near Morlaix, in a week's time! The thing was monstrous. But the south cone was hoisted, and it remained hoisted. And the cone is never displayed except for a real gale,—not a yachtsman's gale, but a sailor's gale, which is serious.

A tender went forth to meet a Dutch American liner in the roads. We followed her along the jetty. At the end of the jetty the gale was already blowing; and rain-squalls were all round the horizon. Soon we were in the midst of a squall ourselves. The rain hid everything for a minute. It cleared. The vast stretch of sands glistened wet, with the variegated bathing-tents, from which even then beautiful creatures were bathing in a shallow surf. Beyond was the casino, and all the complex roofs of Boulogne, and to the north a road climbing up to the cliff-top, and the illimitable dunes that are a feature of this part of the country. Above all floated thunder-clouds, white in steely blue. The skipper did not like those thunder-clouds; he said they were the most dangerous of all clouds, "because anything might come out of them." He spoke as if they already contained in their bosoms every conceivable sort of weather, which they would let loose according to their caprice.

The rain resumed heavily. The wind compelled us to hold tight to the rail of the pier. A poster announced that in the casino behind the rain, Suppé's "Boccaccio" was to be performed that night, and Massenet's "Thaïs" the next night. And opera seemed a very artificial and unnecessary form of activity as we stood out there in the reality of the storm. The Atlantic liner had now bid good-by to the tender, and was hugely moving. She found sea-room, and then turned with the solemnity of her bigness, and headed straight into the gale, pitching like a toy. The rain soon veiled her, and she was gone. I could not picture the *Velsa* in such a

ON THE DUNES NEAR BOULOGNE

situation, at any rate with the owner on board. We went back, rather pensive, to the Quai Chanzy.

The men in the pilot-boat alongside the *Velsa* were not in the least reassuring as to the chances of the *Velsa* ever getting to Brittany; but they were uplifted because the weather was too rough for them to go out. When the cone is on view, the pilot-service is accomplished by a powerful steam-vessel. Our friends, in their apparently happy idleness, sculled forth in a dinghy about fifty yards from where we lay, and almost immediately rejoined us with three eels that they had caught. I bought the three eels for two shillings, and the cook cooked them perfectly, and I ate one of them with ecstasy a few hours later; but eels are excessively antipathetic to the digestive organs, and may jaundice the true bright color of the world for days.

The transaction of the eels strengthened our intimacy with the pilot's crew, who imparted to us many secrets; as, for example, that they were the selfsame men who act as porters at the quay for the transfer of luggage when the cross-channel steamers arrive and depart. On one day they are the pilot's crew, and on the next they are porters to carry your handbags through the customs. This was a blow to me, because on the innumerable occasions when I had employed those porters I had always regarded them as unfortunate beings who could earn money only during about an hour each day, victims of the unjust social system, etc., and who were therefore specially deserving of compassion and tips. I now divined that their activities were multiple, and no doubt dovetailed together like a Chinese puzzle, and all reasonably remunerative. The which was very French and admirable. Herein was a valuable lesson to me, and a clear saving in future of that precious commodity, compassion.

In a day or two the horrid fact emerged that we were imprisoned in Boulogne. The south cone did not budge. Neither could we. The tide ebbed; the tide flowed; we sank softly into the mud; we floated again. A sailor cut our warp because it was in his way, and therefore incurred our anger and the comminations of the harbor-master. But we were not released. An aëroplane meeting was announced, and postponed. We witnessed the preparations for the ceremonial opening of a grand

FOLKESTONE TO BOULOGNE

new dock. We went to the casino and listened to Russian music, which in other circumstances would have enchanted us.

But none of these high matters could hold our attention. Even when the cook criticized our water-colors with faint praise, and stated calmly that he, too, was a water-colorist, and brought proofs of his genius out of the forecastle, even then we were not truly interested. We thirsted to depart, and could not. Our sole solace was to walk round and round the basin in the rain-squalls, and observe their tremendous vitality, which, indeed, never ceased, day or night save at low water, when most craft were aground.

At such periods of tranquillity the trucks of the fishing-smacks were nearly level with the quay, and we noticed that every masthead was elaborately finished with gilded sculpture—a cross, a star, or a small figure of Jesus, the Virgin Mary, or an angel. The names, too, of these smacks were significant: *Resurrection, Jesus-Marie,* and so on. The ornamentation of the deck-houses and companions of these vessels showed a great deal of fantasy and brilliant color, though little taste. And the general effect was not only gay, but agreeable, demonstrating, as it did, that the boats were beloved. English fishing-boats are beloved by their owners, but English affection does not disclose itself in the same way, if it discloses itself at all. On the third afternoon we assisted at the departure of an important boat for the herring fisheries. It had a crew of seventeen men, all dressed in brown, young and old, and an enormous quantity of gear. It bore the air of a noble coöperative enterprise, and went off on the tide, disdainfully passing the still-hoisted cone.

Perhaps it was this event that gave us to think. If a herring-boat could face the gale, why not we? Our ship was very seaworthy, and the coast was dotted with sheltering ports. Only it was impossible to go south, since we could not have made headway. Then why not boldly cancel the rendezvous in Brittany, and run northward before the gale? The skipper saluted the idea with enthusiasm. He spoke of Ostend. He said that if the wind held we could easily run to Ostend in a day. He did not care for Ostend, but it would be a change. I, however, did care for Ostend. And so it was de-

MAKING A DIPLOMATIC EPISODE OUT OF NOTHING AT ALL

FOLKESTONE TO BOULOGNE

cided that, unless the wind went right round in the night, we would clear out of Boulogne at the earliest tidal hour the next morning. The joy of expectancy filled the ship, and I went into the town to buy some of the beautiful meat-pies that are offered in its shops.

CHAPTER XV

TO BELGIUM

AT 6 A. M. we, too, were passing disdainfully the still-hoisted cone. Rain descended in sheets, in blankets, and in curtains, and when we did not happen to be in the rain, we could see rain-squalls of the most theatrical appearance in every quarter of the horizon. The gale had somewhat moderated, but not the sea; the wind, behind us, was against the tide, and considerably quarreling therewith. Now we were inclosed in walls of water, and now we were balanced on the summit of a mountain of water, and had a momentary view of many leagues of tempest. I personally had never been out in such weather in anything smaller than a mail-steamer.

Here I must deal with a distressing subject, which it would be pleasanter to ignore, but which my training in realism will not allow me to ignore. A certain shameful crime is often committed on

TO BELGIUM

yachts, merchantmen, and even men-of-war. It is notorious that Nelson committed this crime again and again, and that other admirals have copied his iniquity. Sailors, and particularly amateur sailors, would sooner be accused of any wickedness rather than this. Charge them with cheating at cards, ruining innocent women, defrauding the Government, and they will not blench; but charge them with this offense, and they will blush, they will recriminate, and they will lie disgracefully against all evidence; they cannot sit still under the mere suspicion of it.

As we slipped out of the harbor that morning the secret preoccupation of the owner and his friend was that circumstances might tempt them to perpetrate the sin of sins. Well, I am able to say that they withstood the awful temptation; but only just! If out of bravado they had attempted to eat their meals in the saloon, the crime would assuredly have been committed, but they had the sense to order the meals to be served in the cockpit, in the rain, in the blast, in the cold. No matter the conditions! They were saved from turpitude, and they ate heartily thrice during the day. And pos-

FROM THE LOG OF THE *VELSA*

sibly nobody was more astonished than themselves at their success in virtue. I have known a yachtsman, an expert, a member of an exceedingly crack club, suddenly shift his course shoreward in circumstances not devoid of danger.

"What are you about?" was the affrighted question. He replied:

"I'm going to beach her. If I don't, I shall be sick, and I won't be sick aboard this yacht."

Such is the astounding influence of convention, which has transformed into a crime a misfortune over which the victim has no control whatever. We did not beach the *Velsa*, nor were our appetites impaired. We were lucky, and merely lucky; and yet we felt as proud as though we had, by our own skill and fortitude, done something to be proud of. This is human nature.

As we rounded Cape Gris-Nez, amid one of the most majestic natural scenes I have ever witnessed, not a gale, but about half of a gale, was blowing. The wind continued to moderate. Off Calais the tide was slack, and between Calais and Dunkirk we had it under our feet, and were able to dispense with the engine and still do six and a half knots

TO BELGIUM

an hour. Thenceforward the weather grew calm with extraordinary rapidity, while the barometer continuously fell. At four o'clock the wind had entirely expired, and we restarted the engine, and crawled past Westend and Nieuport, resorts very ugly in themselves, but seemingly beautiful from the sea. By the time we sighted the whiteness of the kursaal at Ostend the water was as flat as an inland lake. The sea took on the most delicate purple tints, and the pallor of the architecture of Belgian hotels became ethereal. While we were yet a mile and a half from the harbor-mouth, flies with stings wandered out from the city to meet us.

We passed between the pierheads at Ostend at 6:40 P. M., and the skipper was free to speak again. When he had done manœuvering in the basin, he leaned over the engine-hatch and said to me:

"I've had a bit o' luck this week."

"With the engine?" I suggested, for the engine had been behaving itself lately.

"No, sir. My wife presented me with a little boy last Tuesday. I had the letter last night. I've been expecting it." But he had said nothing to me before. He blushed, adding, "I should like you to do me a very great favor, sir—give me two days off soon, so that I can go to the baptism."

Strange, somehow, that a man should have to ask a favor to be present at the baptism of his own son! The skipper now has two sons. Both, I was immediately given to understand, are destined for the sea. He has six brothers-in-law, and they all follow the sea. On a voyage he will never willingly leave the wheel, even if he is not steering. He will rush down to the forecastle for his dinner, swallow it in two minutes and a half, and rush back. I said to him once:

"I believe you must be fond of this wheel."

"I am, sir," he said, and grinned.

We lay nearly opposite the railway station, and our rudder was within a foot of the street. Next to us lay the *Velsa's* sister (occasion for the historic remark that "the world is very small"), a yacht well known to the skipper, of exactly the same lines as the *Velsa,* nearly the same size, and built within four miles of her in the same year! The next morning, which was a Sunday, the sisters were equally drenched in tremendous downpours of rain, but made no complaint to each other. I had the

TO BELGIUM

awning rigged, which enabled us, at any rate, to keep the saloon skylights open.

The rain had no effect on the traditional noisiness of Ostend. Like sundry other cities, Ostend has two individualities, two souls. All that fronts the sea and claims kinship with the kursaal is grandiose, cosmopolitan, insincere, taciturn, blatant, and sterile. It calls itself the finest sea-promenade in Europe, and it may be, but it is as factitious as a meringue. All that faces the docks and canals is Belgian, more than Belgian—Flemish, picturesque, irregular, strident, simple, unaffected, and swarming with children. Narrow streets are full of little cafés that are full of little men and fat women. All the little streets are cobbled, and everything in them produces the maximum quantity of sound. Even the postmen carry horns, and all the dogs drawing little carts bark loudly. Add to this the din of the tram-cars and the whistling of railway engines.

On this Sunday morning there was a band festival of some kind, upon which the pitiless rain had no effect whatever. Band after band swung past our rudder, blaring its uttermost. We had some marketing to do, as the cook declared that he could market neither in French nor Flemish, and we waited impatiently under umbrellas for the procession of bands to finish. It would not finish, and we therefore had to join it. All the way up the Rue de la Chapelle we could not hear ourselves speak in the brazen uproar; and all the brass instruments and all the dark uniforms of the puffy instrumentalists were glittering and melting in the rain. Occasionally at the end of the street, over the sea, lightning feebly flickered against a dark cloud. At last I could turn off into a butcher's shop, where under the eyes of a score of shopping matrons I purchased a lovely piece of beef for the nominal price of three francs seventy-five centimes, and bore it off with pride into the rain.

When we got back to the yacht with well-baptized beef and vegetables and tarts, we met the deck-hand, who was going alone into the interesting and romantic city. Asked what he was about, he replied:

"I'm going to buy a curio, sir; that's all." He knew the city. He had been to Ostend before in a cargo-steamer, and he considered it neither in-

BATHING TENTS AND GIRLS

teresting nor romantic. He pointed over the canal toward the country. "There's a pretty walk over there," he said; "but there's nothing here," pointing to the town. I had been coming to Ostend for twenty years, and enjoying it like a child, but the deck-hand, with one soft-voiced sentence, took it off the map.

In the afternoon, winding about among the soaked cosmopolitanism of the promenade, I was ready to agree with him. Nothing will destroy fashionable affectations more surely than a wet Sunday, and the promenade seemed to rank first in the forlorn tragedies of the world. I returned yet again to the yacht, and was met by the skipper with a disturbed face.

"We can't get any fresh water, sir. Horse isn't allowed to work on Sundays. *Everything's changed in Belgium.*" The skipper was too Dutch to be fond of Flanders. His mightiest passion was rising in him—the passion to go somewhere else.

"All right," I said; "we'll manage with mineral water, and then we'll move on to Bruges." In rain it is, after all, better to be moving than to be standing still.

FROM THE LOG OF THE *VELSA*

But to leave Ostend was not easy, because the railway bridge would not swing for us, nor would it yield, for over an hour, to the song of our siren. Further, the bridge-man deeply insulted the skipper. He said that he was not supposed to swing for *canal-boats*.

"Canal-boat!" the skipper cried. "By what canal do you think I brought this ship across the North Sea?" He was coldly sarcastic, and his sarcasm forced the bridge open. We passed through, set our sails, and were presently heeling over and washing a wave of water up the banks of the canal. I steered, and, as we overtook an enormous barge, I shaved it as close as I could for the fun of the thing. Whereupon the skipper became excited, and said that for a yacht to touch a barge was fatal, because the barges were no stronger than cigar-boxes, having sides only an inch thick, and would crumble at a touch; and the whole barge-population of Belgium and Holland, but especially Belgium, was in a conspiracy to extract damages out of yachts on the slightest pretext. It seemed to me that the skipper's alarm was exaggerated. I understood it a few days later, when he related to

TO BELGIUM

me that he had once quite innocently assisted at the cracking of a cigar-box, for which his employer had had to pay five thousand francs.

The barge which I had failed to sink had two insignificant square-sails set, like pocket-handkerchiefs, but was depending for most of its motion on a family of children who were harnessed to its tow-rope in good order.

Now the barometer began to fall still lower, and simultaneously the weather improved and brightened. It was a strange summer, was that summer! The wind fell, the lee-board ceased to hum pleasantly through the water, and we had to start the engine, which is much less amusing than the sails. And the towers of Bruges would not appear on the horizon of the monotonous tree-lined canal, upon whose banks every little village resembles every other little village. We had to invent something to pass the time, and we were unwise enough to measure the speed of the engine on this smooth water in this unusual calm. A speed trial is nearly always an error of tact, for the reason that it shatters beautiful illusions. I had the beautiful illusion that under favorable conditions the engine would drive the yacht at the rate of twelve kilometers an hour. The canal-bank had small posts at every hundred meters and large posts at every thousand. The first test gave seven and a half kilometers an hour. It was unthinkable. The distances must be wrong. My excellent watch must have become capricious. The next test gave eight kilometers. The skipper administered a tonic to the engine, and we rose to nine, only to fall again to eight. Allowing even that the dinghy took a kilometer an hour off the speed, the result of the test was very humiliating. We crawled. We scarcely moved.

Then, feeling the need of exercise, I said I would go ashore and walk along the bank against the yacht until we could see Bruges. I swore it, and I kept the oath, not with exactitude, but to a few hundred meters; and by the time my bloodshot eyes sighted the memorable belfry of Bruges in the distance, I had decided that the engine was perhaps a better engine than I had fancied. I returned on board, and had to seek my berth in a collapse. Nevertheless the *Velsa* had been a most pleasing object as seen from the bank.

STREET SCENE IN BRUGES

CHAPTER XVI

BRUGES

WE moored at the Quai Spinola, with one of the most picturesque views in Bruges in front of us, an irresistible temptation to the water-colorist, even in wet weather. I had originally visited Bruges about twenty years earlier. It was the first historical and consistently beautiful city I had ever seen, and even now it did not appear to have sunk much in my esteem. It is incomparably superior to Ghent, which is a far more important place, but in which I have never been fortunate. Ghent is gloomy, whereas Bruges is melancholy, a different and a finer attribute. I have had terrible, devastating adventures in the restaurants of Ghent, and the one first-class monument there is the medieval castle of the counts of Flanders, an endless field for sociological speculation, but transcendently ugly and depressing. Ghent is a modern town in an old suit of clothes, and its inhabitants are more formidably Belgian than those of any other large city of Flanders. I speak not of the smaller industrial places, where Belgianism is ferocious and terrible.

At Bruges, water-colors being duly accomplished, we went straight to Notre Dame, where there was just enough light left for us to gaze upon Michelangelo's "Virgin and Child," a major work. Then to the streets and lesser canals. I found changes in the Bruges of my youth. Kinematographs, amid a conflagration of electricity, were to be expected, for no show-city in Europe has been able to keep them out. Do they not enliven and illumine the ground floors of some of the grandest renaissance palaces in Florence? But there were changes more startling than the advent kinematographs. Incandescent gas-mantles had replaced the ordinary burners in the street-lamps of the town! In another fifty years the corporation of Bruges will be using electricity.

Still more remarkable, excursion motor-boats were running on the canals, and at the improvised landing-stages were large signs naming Bruges "The Venice of the North." I admit that my feelings were hurt—not by the motor-boats, but by the signs. Bruges is no more the Venice of the North, than Venice is the Bruges of the South.

We allowed the soft melancholy of Bruges to descend upon us and penetrate us, as the motor-boats ceased to run and the kinematographs grew more brilliant in the deepening night. We had to dine, and all the restaurants of the town were open to us. Impossible to keep away from the Grande Place and the belfry, still incessantly chattering about the time of day. Impossible not to look with an excusable sentimentality at the Hôtel du Panier d'Or, which in youth was the prince of hotels, with the fattest landlord in the world, and thousands of mosquitos ready among its bed-hangings to assist the belfry-chimes in destroying sleep. The Panier d'Or was the only proper hotel for the earnest art-loving tourist who could carry all his luggage and was firmly resolved not to spend more than seven francs a day at the outside. At the Panier d'Or one was sure to encounter other travelers who took both art and life seriously.

No, we would not dine at the Panier d'Or, because we would not disturb our memories. We glanced like ghosts of a past epoch at its exterior, and we slipped into the café restaurant next door, and were served by a postulant boy waiter who had everything to learn about food and human nature, but who was a nice boy. And after dinner, almost saturated with the exquisite melancholy of the Grande Place, we were too enchanted to move. We drank coffee and other things, and lingered until all the white cloths were removed from the tables; and the long, high room became a café simply. A few middle-aged male habitués wandered in separately,—four in all,—and each sat apart and smoked and drank beer. The mournfulness was sweet and overwhelming. It was like chloroform. The reflection that each of these sad, aging men had a home and an *intimité* somewhere in the spacious, transformed, shabby interiors of Bruges, that each was a living soul with aspirations and regrets, this reflection was excruciating in its blend of forlornness and comedy.

A few more habitués entered, and then a Frenchman and a young Frenchwomen appeared on a dais at the back of the café and opened a piano. They were in correct drawing-room costume, with none

SCENE IN GHENT

of the eccentricities of the *café-chantant,* and they produced no effect whatever on the faces or in the gestures of the habitués. They performed. He sang; she sang; he played; she played. Just the common songs and airs of the Parisian music-halls, vulgar, but more inane than vulgar. The young woman was agreeable, with the large, red mouth which is the index of a comfortable, generous, and good-natured disposition. They sang and played a long time. Nobody budged; nobody smiled. Certainly we did not; in a contest of phlegm Englishmen can, it is acknowledged, hold their own. Most of the habitués doggedly read newspapers, but at intervals there was a momentary dull applause. The economic basis of the entertainment was not apparent to us. The prices of food and drink were very moderate, and no collection was made by or on behalf of the artists.

At length, when melancholy ran off us instead of being absorbed, because we had passed the saturation-point, we rose and departed. Yes, incandescent-mantles and motor-boats were not the only changes in Bruges. And in the café adjoining the one we had left a troupe of girls in white were performing gaily to a similar audience of habitués. We glimpsed them through the open door. And in front of the kinematograph a bell was ringing loudly and continuously to invite habitués, and no habitués were responding. It was all extremely mysterious. The chimes of the belfry flung their strident tunes across the sky, and the thought of these and of the habitués gave birth in us to a suspicion that perhaps, after all, Bruges had not changed.

We moved away out of the Grande Place into the maze of Bruges toward the Quai Spinola, our footsteps echoing along empty streets and squares of large houses the fronts of which showed dim and lofty rooms inhabited by the historical past and also no doubt by habitués. And after much wandering I had to admit that I was lost in Bruges, a city which I was supposed to know like my birthplace. And at the corner of a street, beneath an incandescent-mantle, we had to take out a map and unfold it and peer at it just as if we had belonged to the lowest rank of tourists.

As we submitted ourselves to this humiliation, the carillon of the belfry suddenly came to us over

A ROCOCO CHURCH INTERIOR

BRUGES

a quarter of a mile of roofs. Not the clockwork chimes now, but the carillonneur himself playing on the bells, a bravura piece, delicate and brilliant. The effect was ravishing, as different from that of the clockwork chimes as a piano from a barrel-organ. All the magic of Bruges was reawakened in its pristine force. Bruges was no more a hackneyed rendezvous for cheap trippers and amateur painters and poverty-stricken English bourgeois and their attendant chaplains. It was the miraculous Bruges of which I had dreamed before I had ever even seen the place—just that.

Having found out where we were in relation to the Quai Spinola, we folded up the map and went forward. The carillon ceased, and began again, reaching us in snatches over the roofs in the night wind. We passed under the shadows of rococo churches, the façades and interiors of which are alike neglected by those who take their pleasures solely according to the instructions of guide-books, and finally we emerged out of the maze upon a long lake, pale bluish-gray in the gloom. And this lake was set in a frame of pale bluish-gray houses with stepwise gables, and by high towers, and by a ring of gas-lamps, all sleeping darkly. And on the lake floated the *Velsa*, like the phantom of a ship, too lovely to be real, and yet real. It was the most magical thing.

We could scarcely believe that there was our yacht right in the midst of the town. This was the same vessel that only a little earlier had rounded Cape Gris-Nez in a storm, and suffered no damage whatever. Proof enough of the advantage of the barge-build, with a light draft, and heavy leeboards for use with a beam wind when close-hauled. Some yachtsmen, and expert yachtsmen, too, are strongly against the barge. But no ordinary yacht of the *Velsa's* size could have scraped into that lake by the Quai Spinola and provided us with that unique sensation. The *Velsa* might have been designed specially for the background of Bruges. She fitted it with exquisite perfection.

And the shaft of light slanting up from her forecastle hatch rendered her more domestic than the very houses around, which were without exception dark and blind, and might have been abandoned. We went gingerly aboard across the narrow, yielding gangway, and before turning in gazed again

BRUGES

at the silent and still scene. Not easy to credit that a little way off the kinematograph was tintinnabulating for custom, and a Parisian couple singing and playing, and a troupe of white-frocked girls coarsely dancing.

PART V
EAST ANGLIAN ESTUARIES

CHAPTER XVII

EAST ANGLIA

AFTER the exoticism of foreign parts, this chapter is very English. But no island could be more surpassingly strange, romantic, and baffling than this island. I had a doubt about the propriety of using the phrase "East Anglia" in the title. I asked, therefore, three educated people whether the northern part of Essex could be termed East Anglia, according to current usage. One said he did n't know. The next said that East Anglia began only north of the Stour. The third said that East Anglia extended southward as far as anybody considered that it ought to extend southward. He was a true Englishman. I agreed with him. England was not made, but born. It has grown up to a certain extent, and its pleasure is to be full of anomalies, like a human being. It has to be seen to be believed.

Thus, my income tax is assessed in one town,

twelve miles distant. After assessment, particulars of it are forwarded to another town in another county, and the formal demand for payment is made from there; but the actual payment has to be made in a third town, about twenty miles from either of the other two. What renders England wondrous is not such phenomena, but the fact that Englishmen see nothing singular in such phenomena.

East Anglia, including North Essex, is as English as any part of England, and more English than most. Angles took possession of it very early in history, and many of their descendants, full of the original Anglian ideas, still powerfully exist in the counties. And probably no place is more Anglian than Brightlingsea, the principal yachting center on the east coast, and the home port of the *Velsa*. Theoretically and officially, Harwich is the home port of the *Velsa*, but not in practice: we are in England, and it would never do for the theory to accord with the fact. Brightlingsea is not pronounced Brightlingsea, except at railway stations, but Brigglesea or Bricklesea. There is some excuse for this uncertainty, as Dr.

A FISH-RESTAURANT BOAT

EAST ANGLIA

Edward Percival Dickin, the historian of the town, has found 198 different spellings of the name.

Brightlingsea is proud of itself, because it was "a member of the Cinque Ports." Not *one* of the Cinque Ports, of which characteristically there were seven, but a member. A "member" was subordinate, and Brightlingsea was subordinate to Sandwich, Heaven knows why. But it shared in the responsibilities of the Cinque. It helped to provide fifty-seven ships for the king's service every year. In return it shared in the privilege of carrying a canopy over the king at the coronation, and in a few useful exemptions. After it had been a member of the Cinque for many decades and perhaps even centuries, it began to doubt whether, after all, it was a member, and demanded a charter in proof. This was in 1442. The charter was granted, and it leads off with these words: "To all the faithful in Christ, to whom these present letters shall come, the Mayors and Bailiffs of the Cinque Ports, Greeting in the Lord Everlasting." By this time ships had already grown rather large. They carried four masts, of which the aftermost went by the magnificent title of the "bonaventure

FROM THE LOG OF THE *VELSA*

mizen"; in addition they had a mast with a square sail at the extremity of the bow-sprit. They also carried an astrolabe, for the purposes of navigation.

Later, smuggling was an important industry at Brightlingsea, and to suppress it laws were passed making it illegal to construct fast rowing- or sailing-boats. In the same English, and human, way, it was suggested at the beginning of the twentieth century that since fast motor-cars kicked up dust on the roads, the construction of motor-cars capable of traveling fast should be made illegal. There are no four-masted ships now at Brightlingsea; no bowsprit carries a mast; no ship puts to sea with an astrolabe; the "bonaventure mizen" is no more; smuggling is unfashionable; fast craft are encouraged.

Nevertheless, on a summer's morning I have left the *Velsa* in the dinghy and rowed up the St. Osyth Creek out of Brightlingsea, and in ten minutes have been lost all alone between slimy mud banks with a border of pale grass at the top, and the gray English sky overhead, and the whole visible world was exactly as it must have been when the original

EAST ANGLIA

Angles first rowed up that creek. At low water the entire Christian era is reduced to nothing, in many a creek of the Colne, the Blackwater, and the Stour; England is not inhabited; naught has been done; the pristine reigns as perfectly as in the African jungle. And the charm of the scene is indescribable. But to appreciate it one must know what to look for. I was telling an Essex friend of mine about the dreadful flatness of Schleswig-Holstein. He protested. "But are n't you educated up to flats?" he asked. I said I was. He persisted. "But are you educated up to mud, the lovely colors on a mud-flat?" He was a true connoisseur of Essex. The man who is incapable of being ravished by a thin, shallow tidal stream running between two wide, shimmering mud banks that curve through a strictly horizontal marsh, without a tree, without a shrub, without a bird, save an eccentric sea-gull, ought not to go yachting in Essex estuaries.

Brightlingsea is one of the great centers of oyster-fishing, and it catches more sprats than any other port in the island, namely, about fifteen hundred tons of them per annum. But its most spectacular industry has to do with yachting. It began to be a yachting resort only yesterday; that is to say, a mere seventy-five years ago. It has, however, steadily progressed, until now, despite every natural disadvantage and every negligence, it can count a hundred and twenty yachts and some eight hundred men employed therewith. A yacht cannot get into Brightlingsea at all from the high sea without feeling her way among sand-banks,—in old days before bell-buoys and gas-buoys, the inhabitants made a profitable specialty of salving wrecks, —and when a yacht has successfully come down Brightlingsea Reach, which is really the estuary of the River Colne, and has arrived at the mouth of Brightlingsea Creek, her difficulties will multiply.

In the first place, she will always discover that the mouth of the creek is obstructed by barges at anchor. She may easily run aground at the mouth, and when she is in the creek, she may, and probably will, mistake the channel, and pile herself up on a bank known as the Cinders, or the Cindery. Farther in, she may fail to understand that at one spot there is no sufficiency of water except at about a yard and a half from the shore, which has the ap-

EAST ANGLIA

pearance of being flat. Escaping all these perils, she will almost certainly run into something, or something will run into her, or she may entangle herself in the oyster preserves. Yachts, barges, smacks, and floating objects without a name are anchored anywhere and anyhow. There is no order, and no rule, except that a smack always deems a yacht to be a lawful target. The yacht drops her anchor somewhere, and asks for the harbor-master. No harbor-master exists or ever has existed or ever will. Historical tradition—sacred! All craft do as they like, and the craft with the thinnest sides must look to its sides.

Also, the creek has no charm whatever of landscape or seascape. You can see nothing from it except the little red streets of Brightlingsea and the yacht-yards. Nevertheless, by virtue of some secret which is uncomprehended beyond England, it prospers as a center of yachting. Yachts go to it and live in it not by accident or compulsion, but from choice. Yachts seem to like it. Of course it is a wonderful place, because any place where a hundred and twenty yachts foregather must be a wonderful place. The interest of its creek is inexhaustible, once you can reconcile yourself to its primitive Anglianism, which, after all, really harmonizes rather well with the mud-flats of the county.

An advantage of Brightlingsea is that when the weather eastward is dangerously formidable, you can turn your back on the North Sea and go for an exciting cruise up the Colne. A cruise up the Colne is always exciting because you never know when you may be able to return. Even the *Velsa*, which can float on puddles, has gone aground in the middle of the fair and wide Colne. A few miles up are the twin villages of Wivenhoe and Rowhedge, facing each other across the river, both inordinately picturesque, and both given up to the industry of yachting. At Wivenhoe large yachts and even ships are built, and in winter there is always a choice selection of world-famous yachts on the mud, costly and huge gewgaws, with their brass stripped off them, painfully forlorn, stranded in a purgatory between the paradise of last summer and the paradise of the summer to come.

If you are adventurous, you keep on winding along the curved reaches, and as soon as the last

EAST ANGLIA

yacht is out of sight, you are thrown back once more into the pre-Norman era, and there is nothing but a thin, shallow stream, two wide mud banks, and a border of grass at the top of them. This is your world, which you share with a sea-gull or a crow for several miles; and then suddenly you arrive at a concourse of great barges against a quay, and you wonder by what magic they got there, and above the quay rise the towers and steeples of a city that was already ancient when William the Conqueror came to England in the interests of civilization to take up the white man's burden,—Colchester, where more oysters are eaten on a certain night of the year at a single feast than at any other feast on earth. Such is the boast.

But such contrasts as the foregoing do not compare in violence with the contrasts offered by the River Stour, a few miles farther north on the map of England. Harwich is on the Stour, at its mouth, where, in confluence with the River Orwell (which truly *is* in East Anglia) it forms a goodish small harbor. And Harwich, though a tiny town, is a fairly important naval port, and also "a gate of the empire," where steamers go forth for Bel-

FROM THE LOG OF THE *VELSA*

gium, Holland, Denmark, Germany, and Sweden. We came into Harwich Harbor on the tide one magnificent Sunday afternoon, with the sea a bright green and the sky a dangerous purple, and the entrance to the Stour was guarded by two huge battle-ships, the *Blake* and the *Blenheim,* each apparently larger than the whole of the town of Harwich. Up the Stour, in addition to all the Continental steamers, was moored a fleet of forty or fifty men-of-war, of all sorts and sizes, in a quadruple line. It was necessary for the *Velsa* to review this fleet of astoundingly ugly and smart black monsters, and she did so, to the high satisfaction of the fleet, which in the exasperating tedium of Sunday afternoon was thirsting for a distraction, even the mildest. On every sinister ship—the *Basilisk,* the *Harpy,* etc., apposite names!—the young bluejackets (they seemed nearly all to be youths) were trying bravely to amuse themselves. The sound of the jews'-harp and of the concertina was heard, and melancholy songs of love. Little circles of men squatted here and there on the machinery-encumbered decks playing at some game. A few students were reading; some athletes were spar-

BRIGHTLINGSEA CREEK

ring; many others skylarking. None was too busy to stare at our strange lines. Launches and longboats were flitting about full of young men, going on leave to the ecstatic shore joys of Harwich or sadly returning therefrom. Every sound and noise was clearly distinguishable in the stillness of the hot afternoon. And the impression given by the fleet as a whole was that of a vast masculine town, for not a woman could be descried anywhere. It was striking and mournful. When we had got to the end of the fleet I had a wild idea:

"Let us go up the Stour."

At half-flood it looked a noble stream at least half a mile wide, and pointing west in an almost perfect straight line. Nobody on board ever had been up the Stour or knew anybody who had. The skipper said it was a ticklish stream, but he was always ready for an escapade. We proceeded. Not a keel of any kind was ahead. And in a moment, as it seemed, we had quitted civilization and the latest machinery and mankind, and were back in the Anglian period. River marshes, and distant wooded hills, that was all; not even a tilled field in sight! The river showed small headlands, and bights of primeval mud. Some indifferent buoys indicated that a channel existed, but whether they were starboard or port buoys nobody could tell. We guessed, and took no harm. But soon there were no buoys, and we slowed down the engine in apprehension, for on the wide, deceptive waste of smooth water were signs of shallows. We dared not put about, we dared not go ahead. Astern, on the horizon, was the distant fleet, in another world. Ahead, on the horizon, was a hint of the forgotten town of Mistley. Then suddenly a rowboat approached mysteriously out of one of those bights, and it was manned by two men with the air of conspirators.

"D' ye want a pilot?"

We hardened ourselves.

"No."

They rowed round us, critically staring, and receded.

"Why in thunder is n't this river buoyed?" I demanded of the skipper.

The skipper answered that the intention obviously was to avoid taking the bread out of the mouths of local pilots. He put on speed. No catastrophe. The town of Mistley approached us. Then we had to pause again, reversing the propeller. We were in a network of shallows. Far to port could be seen a small red buoy; it was almost on the bank. Impossible that it could indicate the true channel. We went straight ahead and chanced it. The next instant we were hard on the mud in midstream, and the propeller was making a terrific pother astern. We could only wait for the tide to float us off. The rowboat appeared again.

"D' ye want a pilot?"

"No."

And it disappeared.

When we floated, the skipper said to me in a peculiar challenging tone:

"Shall we go on, sir, or shall we return?"

"We'll go on," I said. I could say no less.

We bore away inshore to the red buoy, and, sure enough, the true channel was there, right under the south bank. And we came safely to the town of Mistley, which had never in its existence seen even a torpedo-boat and seldom indeed a yacht, certainly never a *Velsa*. And yet the smoke of the harbor of Harwich was plainly visible from its antique quay. The town of Mistley rose from its secular slumber to enjoy a unique sensation that afternoon.

"Shall we go on to Manningtree, sir?" said the skipper, adding with a grin, "There's only about half an hour left of the flood, and if we get aground again—"

It was another challenge.

"Yes," I said.

Manningtree is a town even more recondite than Mistley, and it marks the very end of the navigable waters of the Stour. It lay hidden round the next corner. We thought we could detect the channel, curving out again now into midstream. We followed the lure, opened out Manningtree the desired—and went on the mud with a most perceptible bump. Out, quick, with the dinghy! Cover her stern-sheets with a protecting cloth, and lower an anchor therein and about fifty fathoms of chain, and row away! We manned the windlass, and dragged the *Velsa* off the mud.

"Shall we go on, sir?"

"No," I said, not a hero. "We'll give up Manningtree this trip." Obstinacy in adventure might have meant twelve hours in the mud. The crew breathed relief. We returned, with great care, to civilization. We knew now why the Stour is a desolate stream. Thus to this day I have never reached Manningtree except in an automobile.

And there are still stranger waters than the Stour; for example, Hamford Water, where explosives are manufactured on lonely marshes, where immemorial wharves decay, and wild ducks and owls intermingle, and public-houses with no public linger on from century to century, and where the saltings are greener than anywhere else on the coast, and the east wind more east, and the mud more vivid. And the *Velsa* has been there, too.

CHAPTER XVIII

IN SUFFOLK

THE Orwell is reputed to have the finest estuary in East Anglia. It is a broad stream, and immediately Shotley Barracks and the engines of destruction have been left behind, it begins to be humane and reassuring. Thanks to the surprising modernity of the town of Ipswich, which has discovered that there are interests more important than those of local pilots, it is thoroughly well buoyed, so that the stranger and the amateur cannot fail to keep in the channel. It insinuates itself into Suffolk in soft and civilized curves, and displays no wildness of any kind and, except at one point, very little mud. When you are navigating the Orwell, you know positively that you are in England. On each side of you modest but gracefully wooded hills slope down with caution to the bank, and you have glimpses of magnificent mansions set in the midst of vast, undulating parks, crisscrossed with perfectly graveled paths that gleam in the sunshine. Everything here is private and sacred, and at the gates of the park lodge-keepers guard not only the paradisiacal acres, but the original ideas that brought the estate into existence.

Feudalism, benevolent and obstinate, flourishes with calm confidence in itself; and even on your yacht's deck you can feel it, and you are awed. For feudalism has been, and still is, a marvelous cohesive force. And it is a solemn thought that within a mile of you may be a hushed drawing-room at whose doors the notion of democracy has been knocking quite in vain for a hundred years. Presently you will hear the sweet and solemn chimes of a tower-clock, sound which seems to spread peace and somnolence over half a county. And as you listen, you cannot but be convinced that the feudal world is august and beautiful, and that it cannot be improved, and that to overthrow it would be a vandalism. That is the estuary of the Orwell and its influence. Your pleasure in it will be unalloyed unless you are so ill-advised as to

FROM THE LOG OF THE *VELSA*

pull off in the dinghy, and try to land in one of the lovely demesnes.

About half-way up the estuary, just after passing several big three-masters moored in midstream and unloading into lighters, you come to Pinmill, renowned among yachtsmen and among painters. Its haven is formed out of the angle of a bend in the river, and the narrowness of the channel at this point brings all the traffic spectacularly close to the yachts at anchor. Here are all manner of yachts, and you are fairly certain to see a friend, and pay or receive a visit of state. And also very probably, if you are on board the *Velsa*, some painter on another yacht will feel bound to put your strange craft into a sketch. And the skipper, who has little partiality for these river scenes, will take the opportunity to go somewhere else on a bicycle. You, too, must go ashore, because Pinmill is an exhibition-village, entirely picturesque, paintable, and English. It is liable to send the foreigner into raptures, and Americans have been known to assert that they could exist there in happiness forever and ever.

I believe that some person or persons in author-

THE DOCK, IPSWICH

IN SUFFOLK

ity offer prizes to the peasantry for the prettiest cottage gardens in Pinmill. It is well; but I should like to see in every picturesque and paintable English village a placard stating the number of happy peasants who sleep more than three in a room, and the number of adult able-bodied males who earn less than threepence an hour. All aspects of the admirable feudal system ought to be made equally apparent. The chimes of the castle-clock speak loud, and need no advertisement; cottage gardens also insist on the traveler's attention, but certain other phenomena are apt to escape it.

The charm of Pinmill is such that you usually decide to remain there over night. In one respect this is a mistake, for the company of yachts is such that your early morning Swedish exercises on deck attract an audience, which produces self-consciousness in the exerciser.

Ipswich closes the estuary of the Orwell, and Ipswich is a genuine town that combines industrialism with the historic sense. No American can afford not to visit it, because its chief hotel has a notorious connection with Mr. Pickwick, and was reproduced entire and life-size at a world's fair in

FROM THE LOG OF THE *VELSA*

the United States. Aware of this important fact, the second-hand furniture and curio-dealers of the town have adopted suitable measures. When they have finished collecting, Americans should go to the docks—as interesting as anything in Ipswich—and see the old custom-house, with its arch, and the gloriously romantic French and Scandinavian three-masters that usually lie for long weeks in the principal basin. Times change. Less than eighty years ago the docks of Ipswich were larger than those of London. And there are men alive and fighting in Ipswich to-day who are determined that as a port Ipswich shall resume something of her ancient position in the world.

Just around the corner from the Orwell estuary, northward, is the estuary of the River Deben. One evening, feeling the need of a little ocean air after the close feudalism of the Orwell, we ran down therefrom to the North Sea, and finding ourselves off Woodbridgehaven, which is at the mouth of the Deben, with a flood-tide under us, we determined to risk the entrance. According to all printed advice, the entrance ought not to be risked without local aid. There is a bank at the mouth, with a

IN SUFFOLK

patch that dries at low water, and within there is another bank. The shoals shift pretty frequently, and, worst of all, the tide runs at the rate of six knots and more. Still, the weather was calm, and the flood only two hours old. We followed the sailing directions, and got in without trouble just as night fell. The rip of the tide was very marked, and the coast-guard who boarded us with a coast-guard's usual curiosity looked at us as though we were either heroes or rash fools, probably the latter.

We dropped anchor for the night, and the next morning explored the estuary, with the tide rising. We soon decided that the perils of this famous river had been exaggerated. There were plenty of beacons,—which, by the way, are continually being shifted as the shoals shift,—and moreover the channel defined itself quite simply, for the reason that the rest of the winding river-bed was dry. We arrived proudly at Woodbridge, drawing all the maritime part of the town to look at us, and we ourselves looked at Woodbridge in a fitting manner, for it is sacred to the memory not of Omar Khayyam, but to much the same person, Edward

FROM THE LOG OF THE *VELSA*

Fitzgerald, who well knew the idiosyncrasies of the Deben. Then it was necessary for us to return, as only for about two hours at each tide is there sufficient water for a yacht to lie at Woodbridge.

The exit from the Deben was a different affair from the incoming. Instead of a clearly defined channel, we saw before us a wide sea. The beacons or perches were still poking up their heads, of course, but they were of no use, since they had nothing to indicate whether they were starboard or port beacons. It is such details that harmonise well with the Old-World air of English estuaries—with the swans, for instance, those eighteenth-century birds that abound on the Deben. We had to take our choice of port or starboard. Heaven guided us. We reached the entrance. The tide was at half-ebb and running like a race; the weather was unreliable. It was folly to proceed. We proceeded. We had got in alone; we would get out alone. We shot past the coast-guard, who bawled after us. We put the two beacons in a line astern, obedient to the sailing directions; but we could not keep them in a line. The tide swirled us away, making naught of the engine. We gave a tremendous bump. Yes, we were assuredly on the bank for at least ten hours, if not forever; if it came on to blow, we might well be wrecked. But no. The ancient *Velsa* seemed to rebound elastically off the traitorous sand, and we were afloat again. In two minutes more we were safe. What the coastguard said is not known to this day. We felt secretly ashamed of our foolishness, but we were sustained by the satisfaction of having deprived more local pilots of their fees.

Still, we were a sobered crew, and at the next river-mouth northward—Orford Haven—we yielded to a base common sense, and signaled for a pilot. The river Ore is more dangerous to enter, and far more peculiar even than the Deben. The desolate spot, where it runs into the sea is well called Shinglestreet, for it is a wilderness of shingles. The tide runs very fast indeed; the bar shifts after every gale, and not more than four feet of water is guaranteed on it. Last and worst, the bottom is hard. It was probably the hardness of the bottom that finally induced us to stoop to a pilot. To run aground on sand is bad, but to run aground on anything of a rocky nature may be fatal. Our signal was simply ignored. Not the slightest symptom anywhere of a pilot. We were creeping in, and we continued to creep in. The skipper sent the deck-hand forward with the pole. He called out seven feet, eight feet, seven feet; but these were Dutch feet, of eleven inches each, because the pole is a Dutch pole. The water was ominous, full of curling crests and unpleasant hollows, as the wind fought the current. The deck-hand called out seven, six, five and a half. We could almost feel the ship bump . . . and then we were over the bar. Needless to say that a pilot immediately hove in sight. We waved him off, though he was an old man with a grievance.

We approached the narrows. We had conquered the worst difficulties by the sole help of the skipper's instinct for a channel, for the beacons were incomprehensible to us; and we imagined that we could get through the narrows into the river proper. But we were mistaken. We had a fair wind, and we set all sails, and the engine was working well; but there was more than a six-knot tide rushing out through those narrows, and we could not get through. We hung in them for about half an hour. Then, imitating the example of a fisherman who had followed us, we just ran her nose into the shingle, with the sails still set, and jumped ashore with a rope. The opportunity to paint a water-color of the *Velsa* under full sail was not to be lost. Also we bought fish and we borrowed knowledge from the fisherman. He informed us that we had not entered by the channel at all; that we were never anywhere near it. He said that the channel had four feet at that hour. Thus we learned that local wisdom is not always omniscience.

After a delay of two hours, we went up the Ore on the slack. The Ore is a very dull river, but it has the pleasing singularity of refusing to quit the ocean. For mile after mile it runs exactly parallel with the North Sea, separated from it only by a narrow strip of shingle. Under another name it all but rejoins the ocean at Aldeburgh, where at length it curves inland. On its banks is Orford, a town more dead than any dead city of the Zuyder Zee, and quite as picturesque and as full of character. The deadness of Orford may be estimated from the fact that it can support a kinematograph

FROM THE LOG OF THE *VELSA*

only three nights a week. It has electric light, but no railway, and the chief attractions are the lofty castle, a fine church, an antique quay, and a large supply of splendid lobsters. It knows not the tourist, and has the air of a natural self-preserving museum.

CHAPTER XIX

THE INCOMPARABLE BLACKWATER

TIME was when I agreed with the popular, and the guide-book, verdict that the Orwell is the finest estuary in these parts; but now that I know it better, I unhesitatingly give the palm to the Blackwater. It is a nobler stream, a true arm of the sea; its moods are more various, its banks wilder, and its atmospheric effects much grander. The defect of it is that it does not gracefully curve. The season for cruising on the Blackwater is September, when the village regattas take place, and the sunrises over leagues of marsh are made wonderful by strange mists.

Last September the *Velsa* came early into Mersea Quarters for Mersea Regatta. The Quarters is the name given to the lake-like creek that is sheltered betwen the mainland and Mersea Island—which is an island only during certain hours of the day. Crowds of small yachts have their home in the Quarters, and the regatta is democratic, a concourse or medley of craft ranging from sailing dinghies up through five-tonners to fishing-smacks, trading-barges converted into barge-yachts, real barge-yachts like ourselves, and an elegant schooner of a hundred tons or so, fully "dressed," and carrying ladies in bright-colored jerseys, to preside over all. The principal events occur in the estuary, but the intimate and amusing events, together with all the river gossip and scandal, are reserved for the seclusion of the Quarters, where a long lane of boats watch the silver-gray, gleaming sky, and wait for the tide to cover the illimitable mud, and listen to the excessively primitive band which has stationed itself on a barge in the middle of the lane.

We managed to get on the mud, but we did that on purpose, to save the trouble of anchoring. Many yachts and even smacks do it not on purpose, and at the wrong state of the tide, too. A genuine yachtsman paid us a visit—one of those men who live solely for yachting, who sail their own yachts in all weathers, and whose foible is to dress like a sailor before the mast or like a longshore loafer—and told us a tale of an amateur who had bought a yacht that had inhabited Mersea Quarters all her life. When the amateur returned from his first cruise in her, he lost his nerve at the entrance to the Quarters, and yelled to a fisherman at anchor in a dinghy, "Which is the channel?" The fisherman, seeing a yacht whose lines had been familiar to him for twenty years, imagined that he was being made fun of. He drawled out, *"You know."* In response to appeals more and more excited he continued to drawl out, *"You know."* At length the truth was conveyed to him, whereupon he drawlingly advised: "Let the old wench alone. Let her alone. *She* 'll find her way in all right."

Regattas like the Mersea are full of tidal stories, because the time has to be passed somehow while the water rises. There was a tale of a smuggler on the mud-flats, pursued in the dead of night by a coast-guardsman. Suddenly the flying smuggler turned round to face the coast-guardsman. "Look here," said he to the coast-guardsman with warning persuasiveness, "you 'd better not come any further. *You do see such wonderful queer things in the newspapers nowadays."* The coast-guardsman, rapidly reflecting upon the truth of this dark saying, accepted the advice, and went home.

The mud-flats have now disappeared, guns begin to go off, and presently the regatta is in full activity. The estuary is dotted far and wide with white, and the din of orchestra and cheering and chatter within the lane of boats in the Quarters is terrific. In these affairs, at a given moment in the afternoon, a pause ensues, when the minor low-comedy events are finished, and before the yachts and smacks competing in the long races have come back. During this pause we escaped out of the Quarters, and proceeded up the river, past Bradwell Creek, where Thames barges lie, and past Tollesbury, with its long pier, while the high tide was still slack. We could not reach Maldon, which is the Mecca of the Blackwater, and we anchored a few miles below that municipal survival, in the wildest part of the river, and watched the sun disappear over vast, flat expanses of water as smooth as oil, with low banks whose distances were enormously enhanced by the customary optical delusions of English weather. Close to us was Osea Island, where an establishment for the ref-

LEAVING MALDON

ormation of drunkards adds to the weird scene an artistic touch of the sinister. From the private jetty of Osea Island two drunkards in process of being reformed gazed at us steadily in the deepening gloom. Then an attendant came down the jetty and lighted its solitary red eye, which joined its stare to that of the inebriates.

Of all the estuary towns, Maldon, at the head of the Blackwater, is the pearl. Its situation on a hill, with a fine tidal lake in front of it, is superb, and the strange thing in its history is that it should not have been honored by the brush of Turner. A thoroughly bad railway service has left Maldon in the eighteenth century for the delight of yachtsmen who are content to see a town decay if only the spectacle affords esthetic pleasure.

There is a lock in the river just below Maldon, leading to the Chelmsford Canal. We used this lock, and found a lock-keeper and lock-house steeped in tradition and the spirit of history. Beyond the lock was a basin in which were hidden two beautiful Scandinavian schooners discharging timber and all the romance of the North. The prospect was so alluring that we decided to voyage on the canal, at any rate as far as the next lock, and we asked the lock-keeper how far off the next lock was. He said curtly:

"Ye can't go up to the next lock."

"Why not?"

"Because there's only two feet of water in this canal. There never was any more."

We animadverted upon the absurdity of a commercial canal, leading to a county town, having a depth of only two feet.

He sharply defended his canal.

"Well," he ended caustically, "it's been going on now for a hundred or a hundred and twenty year like that, and I think it may last another day or two."

We had forgotten that we were within the influences of Maldon, and we apologized.

Later—it was a Sunday of glorious weather—we rowed in the dinghy through the tidal lake into the town. The leisured population of Maldon was afoot in the meadows skirting the lake. A few boats were flitting about. The sole organized amusement was public excursions in open sailing-

THE INCOMPARABLE BLACKWATER

boats. There was a bathing-establishment, but the day being Sunday and the weather hot and everybody anxious to bathe, the place was naturally closed. There ought to have been an open-air concert, but there was not. Upon this scene of a population endeavoring not to be bored, the ancient borough of Maldon looked grandly down from its church-topped hill.

Amid the waterways of the town were spacious timber-yards; and eighteenth-century wharves with wharfinger's residence all complete, as in the antique days, inhabited still, but rotting to pieces; plenty of barges; and one steamer. We thought of Sneek, the restless and indefatigable. I have not yet visited in the *Velsa* any Continental port that did not abound in motor-barges, but in all the East Anglian estuaries together I have so far seen only one motor-barge, and that was at Harwich. English bargemen no doubt find it more dignified to lie in wait for a wind than to go puffing to and fro regardless of wind. Assuredly a Thames barge—said to be the largest craft in the world sailed by a man and a boy—in full course on the Blackwater is a noble vision full of beauty, but it does not utter the final word of enterprise in transport.

The next morning at sunrise we dropped slowly down the river in company with a fleet of fishing-smacks. The misty dawn was incomparable. The distances seemed enormous. The faintest southeast breeze stirred the atmosphere, but not the mirror of the water. All the tints of the pearl were mingled in the dreaming landscape. No prospect anywhere that was not flawlessly beautiful, enchanted with expectation of the day. The unmeasured mud-flats steamed as primevally as they must have steamed two thousand years ago, and herons stood sentry on them as they must have stood then. Incredibly far away, a flash of pure glittering white, a sea-gull! The whole picture was ideal.

At seven o'clock we had reached Goldhanger Creek, beset with curving water-weeds. And the creek appeared to lead into the very arcana of the mist. We anchored, and I rowed to its mouth. A boat sailed in, scarcely moving, scarcely rippling the water, and it was in charge of two old white-haired fishermen. They greeted me.

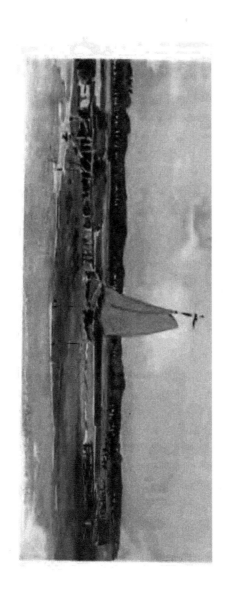